The River's Song

JIM SATTERFIELD

amazon encore

The characters and events portrayed in this book are fictitious. Any similarity to real persons, living or dead, is coincidental and not intended by the author.

Text copyright © 2012 Jim Satterfield
All rights reserved.

Printed in the United States of America.
No part of this book may be reproduced, or stored in a retrieval system, or transmitted in any form or by any means, electronic, mechanical, photocopying, recording, or otherwise, without express written permission of the publisher.

Published by AmazonEncore
P.O. Box 400818
Las Vegas, NV 89140

ISBN-13: 9781612186696
ISBN-10: 1612186696

For Gloria.

Chapter One

Bill Dawkins rose from his blankets and rekindled the fire as the sun cleared the eastern horizon. He looked over at the Miller twins and decided to let them sleep. The last few days had been tough for the young men, especially Ezra. He had lost his fiancée, a beautiful young Métis woman, to a soldier's bullet meant for him and then was arrested by the careless sentries. Dawkins and Jim, Ezra's brother, had busted the heartbroken lad from the army's camp, and now all three were on the run. Not only had they earned the wrath of Colonel Nelson Miles and the entire Fifth Infantry, but their escape route led them right into the middle of hostile Sioux country.

The fire felt good in the crisp prairie air, and Dawkins made coffee and started thinking about breakfast. That, he thought, would get the boys moving, and Dawkins was glad at least they had plenty of grub. It seemed like a lifetime ago when the three of them had left the gold diggings near Helena and struck out for the buffalo country along the Milk River. They had only been out a few months and still had some of the staples they had bought at Fort Benton. Thankfully, along with buffalo meat and the odd deer and elk, food was plentiful.

While sipping his first cup of coffee, Dawkins checked their horses picketed on the edge of camp and found his field glasses

JIM SATTERFIELD

in the wagon that held all his plunder. Not much to show for forty years of hard living, but it was good enough to be beholden to no man and free of the backbreaking work of a miner's life. He was a tall, lean man, deceptively strong and tough from a life of outdoor living, but he prided himself on using his brains and wit more than his fists and weapons to settle trouble.

Dawkins strolled through sagebrush to the rim of the bench overlooking the Milk River Valley, idly glassing for buffalo or other game in the early morning light. The river stretched for miles to the east, meandering through cedar-sprinkled hills and emerald-green meadows before bending out of sight to the north. Deer emerged from the cottonwoods and willows to browse in the hills above the bottomland. Dawkins thought he saw a small herd of buffalo, several miles away, and then realized they were horses. He took a seat on a flat rock, bracing his elbows against his knees to steady the field glasses. Fourteen mounted riders followed the trail made by himself and the Millers. He watched a bit longer and scurried back to the camp.

There he found Jim Miller huddled near the fire, drinking coffee to chase away the morning chill. Dawkins looked over at Ezra, still sleeping, and said to Jim, "Better get your brother going, looks like we got company to the east."

The Miller brothers had been good partners to share a trail. They were young, but hard workers, eager to learn all Dawkins had taught them on the long hunt. They were both tall men, well over six feet, and so identical in appearance it had taken weeks for Dawkins to tell them apart.

Ezra rose before Jim could speak and rubbed his eyes gingerly, taking care not to disturb the bandage on his head. "Soldiers, Bill?"

"Too far to tell, hoss. But that's what I'm thinking. We better git."

THE RIVER'S SONG

Jim pitched his coffee on the ground and rose from the fire. "Bill, show me what you got." The young man, barely twenty, followed Dawkins over to the clearing above the valley floor.

Dawkins found the riders again, who had advanced another quarter of a mile along the wagon trail, and pointed out their location while he passed Jim the field glasses. "I count fourteen riders about three or four miles out, on the far side of the river. They're close to the ford. See 'em?"

"I got 'em. Looks like a squad of cavalry to me by the formation they're in." Jim lowered the glasses and turned to Dawkins.

Dawkins took the glasses and studied the men. "That front rider is probably their wolf, Assiniboine or maybe Crow. Anyways, they're definitely on our trail."

Jim rubbed his hands and blew on his fingers. "How long you s'pose we got?"

"Shoot, a blind man could follow those tracks. They might get slowed a bit when they hit that shale on the other side of the river, but not for long. I'd say we got 'bout an hour on 'em, at best."

Dawkins hurried back to the camp and saw Ezra had already saddled the horses and hitched the wagon. "Ezra, you feel up to ridin'?"

"I reckon so, 'specially if it means keepin' my neck out of a hangman's noose."

Dawkins grimaced. "Just how bad did you hurt that guard, anyway?"

"Bill, when that blue belly shot Belle, I let him have everything I had. All I remember is wringing his neck with both hands until somebody thumped my head. Then all I saw was stars."

"Well, they're coming, either 'cause you killed him or just out of principle." Dawkins hurried about camp, packing his bedding and other equipment into the wagon.

Within ten minutes the men had their gear loaded, and Dawkins climbed up on the wagon bench. "Stay close and scout me a path up to the top of this plateau, then we'll find them riders again."

It only took half an hour to reach the crest of the ridge overlooking the broad Milk River Valley. They followed an old buffalo trail that traversed the steep, brushy hillside and switched back three or four times leading to a wide table where they dismounted and rested the horses. Dawkins jumped down from the wagon and walked a ways with the Millers in tow until he found a point where he had a view of the valley floor below. "They've crossed the river. They're on our side now, and they're still hard on that wagon trail." Dawkins pointed, and handed Jim the field glasses.

"I see 'em. They're movin' fast, probably only a mile or so from the foot of this hill." Jim passed Ezra the glasses. "What now, Bill?"

Dawkins thought out loud, "We ain't gonna outrun 'em, not with this wagon." He looked behind them and pointed to a rocky, low-lying range of hills and badlands. "That country's called the Larb Hills, and it's plenty rough. They'd have a time finding us there." Dawkins paused and rubbed his chin.

Ezra lowered the field glasses. "What's wrong?"

Dawkins looked back toward the wagon. "I don't see any way around splitting up, at least for now."

"I don't know," said Jim, shaking his head, "the odds are long enough already, now we're gonna split up?" Jim took the glasses from Ezra and studied the riders. "They're glued to that trail and they're eatin' up ground. What's your plan, Bill?"

"I thought about just leavin' the wagon behind, but we're gonna need to sell it and our hides to get a stake for headin' west to California."

"None of it's gonna matter much if them soldiers catch us." Ezra nodded toward the approaching riders.

Dawkins looked away from the edge of the plateau and pointed south. "Boys, I want you to leave me here with one of the horses and head toward the Missouri. It'll be about fifty, sixty miles. With a little luck, I'll catch up to you in a couple of days."

"What are you gonna do?" Jim looked back at the riders, who had nearly reached the base of the escarpment.

Dawkins walked to the wagon and climbed into the box. He fetched one of the Sharps rifles, along with a belt of ammunition and his shooting sticks. "I'm gonna wait here and give them bluecoats a proper greeting." Dawkins pointed down toward their campsite that lay around a quarter of a mile below. "I figure in about half an hour, our guests will be riding into our old camp like they own the place. I aim to slow 'em down, buy you boys a head start."

Jim nodded, then climbed up to the wagon bench.

Ezra glanced quickly from Dawkins to Jim. "This is all mostly my doin'. Maybe I ought to just ride down there and give myself up, get you two off the hook."

"It ain't your fault those soldiers treated them Red River folks so badly, taking all their property and shootin' your gal," said Dawkins. "Like it or not, we're all up to our necks in this mess now."

Ezra mounted his horse and looked south. "We better get movin' then."

"Just head for the river, quick as you can. Don't worry 'bout me. I'll be along." Dawkins took his rifle and led his horse to the point overlooking the hillside. He tied his mount a few yards behind the edge of the ridge to a chest-high sagebrush and tested the bowknot with a couple of sharp tugs.

Dawkins hid behind the rim that rose above their old camp below. He pulled his battered Hamilton from his pants and noted the time. Looking over his shoulder, he smiled to see the Millers crest the first wave of ridges that ran all the way down to the Missouri. Then he raised his field glasses and searched for the riders he expected to soon appear at the base of the hill. He did not spot any horses, but he saw where their tracks left the flat prairie and turned uphill toward the first low ridge.

While Dawkins waited, he pondered how to reach Fort Benton, where he hoped to sell their hides and the wagon. He could hail one of the freighters steaming up river to the headwaters of the Missouri. From where they figured to hit the river, around the U bend, it wouldn't be more than a couple of hundred river miles to the fort. If they raised a stake there, it would not be much of a trick to lose anybody looking for them by heading west to the Divide country.

Dawkins heard the riders before he saw them, and he inspected the base of the ridge where the old wagon tracks led to the prairie. Soon a single horseman appeared in the field of his glasses. The man did not look to be a soldier, nor an Indian scout. While Dawkins sized him up, the lead riders of the column appeared, definitely cavalry from their dress and accoutrements. They paused at the base of the escarpment, a thousand yards away. The scout and the commander of the column were having quite a discussion, as Dawkins could see the civilian wildly waving his arm up toward the rocky hillside

THE RIVER'S SONG

in the direction of the bench where the campsite lay. After a few minutes, the scout rode on with the column of soldiers hanging back, maybe a hundred yards.

Dawkins dropped a cartridge into the breech of the rifle and snapped the lever shut. In one fluid motion, he placed it in the crotch of the shooting sticks and knelt into a steady shooting position. Shouldering the buttstock, he peered through the tang sight and took a bead on the campsite, where the riders would soon appear. The rifle was an 1874 Sharps in .44-77, bought new that spring from Holter's Hardware in Helena, along with a second, identical gun back in the wagon. Dawkins figured he had killed at least a thousand buffalo with it over the summer, hunting with the friendly Métis. Between soldiering and hunting, he knew his way around a rifle.

The scout had just about reached the bench, and the cavalrymen were tightening up the ranks. All the riders were in single file as they came out of the brush and rode into the clearing. Dawkins heard a soldier order, "Dismount," and four men handled all the horses, while the rest stretched or relieved themselves in the brush.

Dawkins pushed the butt of the rifle into his armpit and spied the men with his field glasses. The cavalry commander appeared to be young from his lean build and limber gait. Dawkins thought he could make out the shoulder patches of an officer on his blue shirt. He towered over the short, husky civilian who had removed his hat, revealing a shiny, bald pate. Dawkins heard arguing, but could not make out what they were saying. The scout seemed to be doing most of the talking and repeatedly pointed toward the top of the ridge.

Dawkins studied around the old campsite and noticed large, round boulders close to where the horses stood. He raised his rifle and aimed at the biggest rock, allowing for the range, angle, and slight breeze coming from the west. He cocked the hammer and pulled the rear trigger of the rifle, setting the front trigger to release with only a few ounces of pressure. Then he took a deep breath, exhaled about half of it, and slowly squeezed the trigger.

Dawkins heard the bullet strike the boulder before he recovered from the recoil. Soldiers hollered, and several mounts pulled loose from their handlers and galloped back toward the valley. Dawkins quickly reloaded and fired again at another rock near the remaining horses. More mayhem followed and another bunch of riderless horses bolted away from the troopers. Dawkins fired once more and circled around fifty yards to the right to avoid the scattered gunfire of the soldiers.

Creeping to the edge of the ridge, Dawkins peered below and saw only three horses remaining. One of the troopers managed to mount a terrified sorrel and rode downhill after the stampeding horses. Two other soldiers struggled to control their mounts and soon followed after the first rider. The rest of the men had scattered among the rocks and whatever cover they could find. Dawkins reloaded his rifle and looked for another likely target.

Chapter Two

US Deputy Marshal John X. Beidler raised his head ever so slightly to locate the source of the gunfire that had scattered his escorts' horses, rendering the green troopers into a state of panic. He knelt behind a small boulder and scanned the ridgeline, guessing the distance to be at least five hundred yards. "Lieutenant, tell your men to hold their fire," barked Beidler. "They're just wastin' ammo at this range."

He saw a puff of smoke along the ridge, and an instant later a bullet splattered against a boulder to his left, sending bits of rock and lead all around the men. One of the soldiers panicked and ran downhill toward the valley floor. "Men, just stay tight. If he meant to kill you, you'd be dead now." Beidler hollered at the lieutenant, "Control your men or I will, Craft."

Beidler knew all too well Lieutenant William Craft had never seen combat, having graduated from West Point only a few months earlier. The young lieutenant commanded the ragtag column of mounted infantry General Miles assigned to assist in apprehending the men who stole into the army camp near Rock Creek and embarrassed the brass by freeing a prisoner. Beidler had a say in the matter since it was presumed to be civilians they were chasing.

Another shot came from the ridge, but fifty yards or so from the last round, whistling harmlessly over the men, yet still terrifying the soldiers. "Sweet Mary," hollered a young private in a thick brogue, "how many of them are up thar?"

Lieutenant Craft crawled to a rock beside Beidler and whispered hoarsely, "Marshal, what's the strength of the force we're up against?"

Beidler looked with disdain at the young shavetail. "I'm guessing that there's only one man up there." He paused and added, "We'd have overrun him by now, if you'd followed my advice to move up this hill instead of stopping here."

One more shot echoed from the ridge, and a bullet ricocheted off the boulder Beidler and Craft used for cover. Both men dropped to the ground and the lieutenant scoffed, "For only one man, he's sure causing a lot of trouble."

"He can shoot. I'll give you that," said Beidler, "but if we can back off this hillside, we shouldn't have any trouble flanking him."

"How am I supposed to accomplish that maneuver without losing any of my men, Marshal?"

"Tell your men to skedaddle all at once down to the valley." Beidler sneaked a quick glance at the ridge before looking into the lieutenant's terrified eyes. "Whoever that is up there, he's not out for blood. He's stalling for time. Have your men crawl off this hillside now, or I'll give the order myself."

By midday, Beidler and the soldiers squirmed through the last of the rocks and sagebrush on the steep hillside and reached a short knoll sheltering them from the rifleman above. The shooter continued to fire the occasional shot, but it was clear he did not intend to hit any of the men. Beidler rose to his feet for the first time in hours and surveyed the situation.

Nine privates and Lieutenant Craft were accounted for and bent over, catching their wind and rubbing the knots out of their legs. The only noncommissioned officers in the column—a buck sergeant and two corporals—had taken off after the spooked horses, and they were nowhere in sight. Beidler shook his head and thought he would have been better off just taking a couple of men instead of having to wet-nurse this raggedy bunch of mounted infantrymen.

He had heard stories about the Missouri Depot recruits who joined General Miles's column at Fort Peck for the Sitting Bull campaign back in July. They could not shoot and they could not ride, but otherwise they were fine soldiers. *Figures the Old Man would give them to me,* Beidler thought as he tried to come up with a plan to get back on the trail of the fugitives who had led him to this godforsaken part of the Territory. *If things get too tight, I'll just leave these fools behind.*

"Lieutenant, we need to drop down to the river, yonder, and water these men." Beidler was not sure he had Craft's attention, so he stepped closer to the young officer, and spoke in a hushed but threatening tone, "Lieutenant, you do as I tell you and there's just a chance I might be able to get you out of this mess. Remember, you're the one who has to answer to the general."

Craft looked about as if he did not want to share the conversation with his command and spoke in a low voice, "I'm sorry, Marshal, but I've never been shot at before."

Beidler just shook his head. "Yes, well, it comes with the job. Didn't they tell you about that at the Point?" Before Craft could answer, Beidler pointed to the river bottom. "Let's get these men out of the hot sun until Sergeant Jones and the others return with our horses." The marshal did not wait for a response from Craft, as he turned his back on the young man and started walking downhill to the Milk.

While ambling to the river, Beidler made a plan to flank whoever it was that had flushed and unnerved the green cavalry column like so many prairie chickens. He glanced back a time or two as he walked and noticed a shoulder running from the top of the ridge down to the valley floor, a half mile upstream from the morning's ambush. If the men used the cover of that ridge to reach the plateau, they would be nearly on top of the shooter. This looked like a deliberate rearguard action to Beidler, and he knew he needed to lodge that man out of there quickly so they could pursue the rest of the gang.

By Beidler's watch, it was a little past 4:00 p.m. when Sergeant Jones and the two corporals finally appeared to the east with the column's mounts. Beidler had already advised the lieutenant on how to pursue the sharpshooter and now was even less confident in Craft's ability to lead the men. Beidler was no stranger to leading disorganized mobs like this column, though. He had been in pursuit of criminals since the early sixties, when he helped organize the vigilantes around Virginia City. Folks had always underestimated him since he was not even as tall as the shotgun he carried. But he was always where he needed to be and he always did his duty, even if it meant harming a few innocent folks along the way.

This shavetail lieutenant, though, was just dumb enough to think he was really in charge of the chase for these outlaws. He would humor Craft as much as possible, but Beidler was not going to let him get in the way of catching this crew of misfits. He had something to prove to Miles and the rest of that snotty

THE RIVER'S SONG

army brass who had sent him on this fool's errand. These outlaws had attacked a soldier, maybe even killed him, and now Beidler was going to have to clean up the mess, even if that meant lining out this idiot officer.

As Jones and the others arrived at the edge of the cottonwoods with the fugitive horses, Beidler approached the lieutenant and squeezed his upper arm. "We need to move, now. Let's clear that ridge and catch that son-of-a-buck."

Craft looked confused and uncertain. "Shouldn't we rest the horses a bit, perhaps water them before we ride up there, Marshal?"

Beidler was nearing the end of his patience. "Lieutenant," he snarled, "it's past four in the afternoon. Those outlaws have already gained nearly a full day's head start on us. I'm not sure yet where they're headed, but we have got to move or we could lose them in those badlands."

"Yes, I understand, but it's been a very hot day, and that's going to be a hard go up that escarpment—"

"Lieutenant! We've got another four, five hours of good daylight. There's plenty of water back in those hills. We have got to start after them, now!"

Craft closed his eyes and rubbed his forehead. "I just want to think this through, do what's best for my men."

"Your men will do their duty, but they expect their officers to lead by example." Beidler glanced at his watch again. "You crazy fool, I've tried to help you all I can, but I'm riding out now, with or without you."

Craft nodded with little expression and called over his shoulder to Jones, "Sergeant, assemble the column. We're moving out."

Beidler led the men up the valley at a trot for a mile before he turned the column to the left and ascended the long hillside rising to the plateau above. Riding up the slope, Beidler studied the ridges he thought would conceal their movement from the rifleman. If the man had stayed where he had sprung the ambush, he would not be able to see their approach up the hill. Beidler hoped they could reach the top without being fired on. He had already seen for himself how this group of men reacted to gunfire.

Beidler was grateful for the clear sky. It was hot as blue blazes, which was better than the gumbo that would come from a good rain. It would slow the men they were chasing as well, especially with the heavily loaded wagon they had, but they could always abandon that encumbrance, and rain would wash away their tracks, making it nearly impossible to find them. As long as the weather held, he had to push these soldiers.

When the column reached the top of the plateau, Beidler stopped and suggested Craft give the horses a blow. He walked his black mare over to the privates handling the horses. "You men learned your lesson this morning. I don't expect you to lose these mounts again unless you're shot dead." He handed his reins to a young soldier and motioned to Craft. "Lieutenant, grab your field glasses, and let's take a look over the ridge to our left. We might be able to spot our man from there."

Beidler moved carefully to the low-lying shoulder, bending down as he reached the top. He took a knee to avoid skylining himself and was shocked to see Craft rush past him toward the top of the hill, oblivious to the need to remain concealed. "Good grief, man," Beidler hissed. "Get your ass down before whoever's over there sees you."

Craft dropped to his knees and winced. "I'm sorry."

Beidler shook his head in disgust. "Let's just look to the east, see if we can't spot our man. If we don't have any luck, we'll move along to the next ridge. He should be out there within about a mile, if he hasn't taken off." Beidler lay on his belly and crawled to the edge of the rim. He rested on his elbows and methodically studied the broken ground, looking for anything that did not belong.

After only a few minutes, Craft spoke in too loud a voice, "I don't see a thing, Marshal. Maybe we ought to move ahead."

"Hold on, now, Lieutenant, it takes awhile to cover this much country." Beidler viewed the first valley in front of them and started to scan as much of the next ridge as he could. "Lieutenant! Look over to the second ridge yonder. See 'em?"

Craft fumbled with his field glasses, "What have you got?"

"Looks like about fifteen, no, make that twenty Indians coming across that ridgeline, right in our direction."

Chapter Three

Dawkins hid near the top of a rock-strewn hill. He saw for miles across the vast plateau below him, where the fight would soon begin. He had left the ridge where he ambushed the soldiers, shortly after they retreated to the river bottom. Dawkins guessed they would try to flank him, so he had moved up valley a half mile and waited for the column to climb the escarpment.

He spotted the band of Indians coming from the south right after he climbed the hill. He did not think they had seen him, though, because he had been watching them for over an hour and they had not altered their course, nor given any indication they knew they were being watched.

Dawkins guessed they were a Sioux hunting party, judging from their northerly route. He counted at least twenty warriors and noticed some of their ponies dragging travois. They were probably bringing meat back to their camp, somewhere north of the border along Frenchman Creek. Being a hunting party in hostile territory full of General Nelson's soldiers, they would likely be glad just to get back to Canada.

But one could never tell with Sioux.

Dawkins spotted the squad by accident while spying on the Indian party. He saw a man skyline himself on a ridge a mile to the east. He looked beyond the ridge and counted fourteen horses. It had to be the same column he had ambushed that morning.

Dawkins was certain the Sioux had also spotted the soldiers. The warriors bunched up, likely to confer and make a plan. Then they moved to flank the soldiers by riding to the north, toward the edge of the plateau. Dawkins figured the Sioux did not want the soldiers to get between them and the Milk. If these Indians belonged to Sitting Bull's band, they would make sure they could flee to the north and not get trapped below the border. The only question now seemed to be whether the warriors were going to attack the column or slip out of there.

Dawkins guessed they would attack. They outnumbered the soldiers and had to be emboldened by the lack of cohesiveness the squad showed. So far, all Dawkins had seen the soldiers do was assume a defensive position behind a low swale, where they could be easily surrounded by the warriors.

It felt strange for the Sioux to be unwitting allies to him. While Dawkins feared for the soldiers, at the same time he realized how much aid the Indians could be in helping him escape.

He checked his horse, tied in the shade of a canyon cedar. He aimed to watch this mess unfold, then circle to the south away from the Sioux and the soldiers. It was after 6:00 p.m., and he had about three hours of light left. With a little luck, he would cut Jim and Ezra's trail by dark and catch up with them sometime tomorrow.

Dawkins returned his attention to the Indians and saw they were drawing closer to the soldiers, who remained in the same spot. Several warriors appeared to be within rifle range, safely hidden behind a ridge. While Dawkins studied their movement, he saw small plumes of white smoke appear from the soldiers' position. An instant later, he heard gunfire and knew the fight had begun.

Once the shooting started, the Indians began to circle the soldiers' position at the side of a small hill. The soldiers were dismounted and positioned in a skirmish line, with four horse handlers in the rear. Dawkins immediately recognized the folly of their strategy. If some of the Sioux warriors came over the back of the hillside, the horses would be lost and the entire column overrun.

Dawkins figured it was time to ride away. He sidestepped down to his mount and listened to the rising gunfire before he saddled up. "I can't do it," he softly said himself. A delay would cost daylight, and perhaps a chance to escape. But he knew he could not leave that lost column to be butchered by the Sioux, not having once worn blue himself.

Beidler knelt behind one of the rocks scattered about the column's position and hollered over the din of gunfire, "Lieutenant, tell your men to conserve their ammunition! Those Sioux aren't giving us much to shoot at."

He could scarcely believe the turn of events that had unfolded over the last few minutes. One moment he was scanning the ridge for the sharpshooter, and the next thing he knew, the column had engaged a Sioux hunting party. It did not help that that greenhorn, Lieutenant Craft, had revealed their presence to the hostiles by skylining himself. Maybe they could have avoided this mess if they had remained concealed from the Sioux. Too late to worry on that now, though, Beidler realized as he looked about the scattered infantrymen and noted two men sprawled on the ground, wounded or dead.

THE RIVER'S SONG

Craft ducked from rock to rock and slid next to Beidler. "Marshal, we need to get out of here, make a dash for the river below."

Beidler took his eyes off the Sioux warriors riding back and forth in a large arc, just out of good rifle range. "That is the last thing you want to do," he hissed. "We're outnumbered, you fool. If we mount up, they'll run us down and cut us to pieces, especially with the raw recruits you have. Besides, what about your wounded?"

"What should we do, then?" Craft breathed hard, his face drained and pale. "We can't stay here!"

Beidler looked behind their position, then back to the wild-eyed lieutenant. "Stay calm and tell your men not to shoot unless one of them bucks makes a charge for us. We need to watch for any of 'em trying to sneak behind this hill." Beidler grabbed Craft's arm. "Now go give the order not to shoot unless one of them approaches within good shootin' range, then all your men should direct a volley his way."

Beidler watched Craft scurry back to his men and pass along the order. He figured they had a strong enough position to hold off the Sioux from the front, but he did not know how they could stop them circling and attacking from behind.

Dawkins tied his horse to a sagebrush and crawled up to the edge of a knoll overlooking the fight to the west. He scanned the bench below and saw the soldiers holding their own against the Sioux. Three riderless ponies milled about, and he decided some of those soldiers could shoot after all. It was hard to tell if the column had suffered any casualties because they were still dismounted and clinging to the side of the hill. The sun was only a hand or two above the western horizon, and he was surprised the Indians had not yet flanked the soldiers' rear.

Dawkins took a knee behind a waist-high rock and rested the Sharps in the leather fold of his shooting sticks. He placed his jacket and ammunition belt on the ground. He did not want to risk more than two or three shots before he scooted out of there.

From his elevated position along the flank of the fight, Dawkins saw behind the hill where the soldiers had made their stand. He estimated the range to be eight hundred yards. A mighty far piece, but not the longest shot he had ever made.

The fight had slowed, with the Indians withdrawing beyond range of the soldiers. The warriors, now mounted, appeared to be planning their next move. Soon they attacked once more, but half of the warriors circled out of range behind the soldiers. Dawkins watched the Indians turn toward the base of the hill as soon as they were out of the soldiers' view. He loaded his rifle and waited for them to reach the knoll.

Within minutes, half a dozen mounted warriors approached the back of the hill. When they were around fifty yards away, they leaped from their ponies and ran to the foot of the knoll. Dawkins knelt, resting his rifle on the shooting sticks. He raised his rear sight as high as it would go and cocked the Sharps. The rifle seemed to steady itself, and Dawkins peered through the sights to take a bead.

The warriors slowly crept up the rise. From the side, they did not present much of a target to Dawkins. He remembered his father teaching him to shoot when he was a boy in Pennsylvania. "Don't fire at the whole flock," Papa said. "Pick a target." But this was for blood, and any hit was a good shot. Dawkins allowed for range and a gentle breeze. Then he fired at the Indian nearest the crest of the hill.

When Dawkins recovered from the rifle's recoil, he saw one of the Indians at the foot of the knoll fall and thrash about the ground. Two warriors helped the wounded man back to his horse, while the rest of the Sioux looked around in nervous glances, trying to locate the source of the shot.

Dawkins reloaded and aimed at another man, but adjusted his aim several feet higher. Another warrior fell at the shot, and the rest of the Sioux dropped to the ground.

Beidler spied on the location of the Sioux in front of the column through his field glasses, wondering if the rest of the warriors would try to flank them. The warriors had dismounted and were sniping at the men from whatever cover they could find. He lowered his glasses and was shocked to see a puff of gunsmoke rise from a tall hill to his left.

Beidler kept his eye on the hill and saw two more plumes of smoke rise from behind the crest. Then he looked ahead to the Sioux facing them. They did not seem to be aware of the threat to their flank, as Beidler did not see any Indians attempt to approach the hill or reinforce the warriors who had tried to flank them.

A moment later, another cloud of smoke appeared and this time Beidler could hear the shot. "By George, there's a shooter on that ridge covering our rear," he muttered to himself. Beidler looked down the line of soldiers to his right and hollered, "Lieutenant! Slip over here."

Between shots from the warriors facing them, Craft crawled to Beidler's position. "What have you got?" The young lieutenant looked too tired to be scared, with his bloodshot eyes and face slack with fatigue.

"In a few minutes," Beidler hollered over the gunfire, "those Sioux who rode around our flank are going to come back to join the warriors to our front."

Craft gave Beidler an inquisitive look. "How do you figure that, Marshal?"

"Never mind that!" snapped Beidler. "Just listen. If those Indians come back from our right to join their friends, tell your men to really pour it on them."

"I don't know," said Craft. "I've been wondering why those Sioux that peeled around us awhile ago haven't attacked yet."

"I got a hunch, is all." Beidler pointed toward the line of soldiers. "Just go tell your men to look for those Sioux to come back. When they do, let 'em have it."

Craft crawled back down the line, passing along Beidler's instructions. No sooner had he spread the word than ten or twelve mounted warriors appeared within range to their right. The soldiers were ready for them and fired a volley that knocked two men off their horses. In the confusion that followed, the warriors in front retreated to their mounts, and within minutes the entire band headed off the plateau and toward the Milk River in the fading light.

The soldiers rose from the ground cheering and shouting taunts at the Sioux. Craft startled Beidler by giving him a slap on the back. "Hallelujah, Marshal! We ran 'em off! We whipped 'em!"

Beidler allowed a slight grin, but looked toward the tall hill to the left. "That we did, Lieutenant, that we did."

Dawkins rode into darkness. He headed southeast, looking for fresh-cut wagon tracks that would be the Millers', traveling toward the Missouri. No telling how far they would have gotten with a day's head start, but Dawkins did not count on catching up with them until late the next day at best. He was tired and planned on bivouacking as soon as he found their trail.

Half a moon crested the eastern horizon, lighting the plateau and casting shadows here and there behind the cedars and sagebrush. A wolf howled behind him, and a light westerly breeze rustled the prairie grass. There was no need to hurry. Dawkins did not expect to be pursued by the cavalry. Not until morning, at least.

He wondered if the soldiers even knew he had guarded their flank in the skirmish. It did not matter, though. Dawkins counted on them coming, but they would need time to regroup, especially if they had wounded or dead. Dawkins knew the Sioux had casualties, but they would be loaded on the travois, along with their meat, and dragged across the border. He wondered if the soldiers would pursue him or the Sioux.

Dawkins made out wagon tracks in the dim moonlight and veered right to follow the trail. Riding on, he came to a shallow draw where a creek gurgled from one small pool to another. He saw tracks in the streamside grass where the Millers had parked and filled their canteens. Dawkins swung down off his horse and tied it to a stunted cottonwood. He unsaddled Ezra's mare and patted her forehead. "I'll water you directly, girl, but no grazing tonight. Got to keep you near."

Dawkins untied the bedroll from the saddle and unrolled it on a flat piece of ground without rocks or prickly pear cactus. He walked down to the creek and filled his canteen after drinking from the pool. He moseyed back to the mare and led her to the stream. After he watered the horse, he tied her off to a picket line, stretching a lariat between two trees.

Returning to his bed, Dawkins rustled through Ezra's saddlebags and found some Métis pemmican in a small parfleche. He sat on the bed, leaning against the saddle and eating the mixture of dried buffalo meat and berries. It was not half-bad, washed down with cool creek water. Dawkins allowed himself the luxury of removing his boots and slipped between the double-folded blanket.

With his gun belt slung over the saddle horn, Dawkins felt for the Sharps, half-covered in the short scabbard, alongside his bed. No fire this night, just a cold camp, but the evening was clear and warm. He rested his head and listened to the night sounds as he gazed into the diamond-studded sky.

His mother had taught him the stars and constellations when he was a boy, back home in Pennsylvania. She used to sit with him in the dark and point to the Scorpion, or Hercules, and trace the outline of the figures for him while fireflies glowed and bullfrogs croaked in the millpond. He wished she had seen the western skies. More stars than a body could count.

The mare neighed, and downstream in a little grove of cottonwoods, an owl hooted. Now and then, a noisy pack of coyotes yipped and whined and barked. Dawkins's eyes grew heavy, and soon he dreamed of a small farm in a green, fertile valley from a long time ago.

Chapter Four

Beidler was up before first light, rolling his bed and packing his gear. He had outlaws to chase, and he was not getting any closer by sitting in camp. When he walked over to where the horses were picketed, he was stunned to find the sentry asleep. Beidler slipped behind the man and thrashed him with a stick, springing the soldier to life. "Damn it, man!" snorted Beidler. "I ought to have you shot."

The commotion woke Lieutenant Craft, who snapped out of bed. "Marshal, where're you headed?" Craft tipped over his boots to dump out any vermin that might have found themselves a home, then pulled them on.

"Lieutenant, you've got wounded to care for." Beidler nodded toward a lean-to the men had raised for the two soldiers shot by the Sioux. "I think those men will make it, but you'll need to build a couple of travois to get 'em back to the main camp on the Milk."

Craft ambled over to where Beidler was packing the last of his equipment. "I don't know, Marshal. Maybe you ought to come back with us."

"You'll be all right, Lieutenant," Beidler said. "Have a couple of men drop down into that draw to the east and fetch timber for the travois."

Craft looked more bewildered than normal, with his shaggy, blond hair pointing everywhere and his eyes puffy with sleep. "What about going after those Sioux, Marshal?" Craft looked to the north. "They'd be easy to trail, dragging those travois with their wounded."

Beidler laughed and stood, his bedroll tucked under one arm. "Those Indians are long gone, Lieutenant. Shoot, I'd say they're in Canada by now, or close to it." Beidler shook his head. "You all best just get on back to the main command."

"How many of my men are you going to be taking with you?"

"None."

"You're taking off after those men alone?"

"Your men just slow me down, Lieutenant," Beidler said. "Believe me, I've chased after a lot more dangerous men than these by myself. And I've always got the job done."

Craft turned and walked over to his sergeant and conferred with him out of Beidler's hearing. A moment later, he came back to where Beidler saddled his horse. "Hold on, Marshal," said Craft. "Give me a few minutes to get my things ready. I'm coming with you."

"That's the last thing I need, Craft," snapped Beidler, looking up to the young shavetail who stood at least a foot taller than he.

"Say what you will, but the army has an interest in this matter, and I'm coming," said Craft. "Sergeant Jones can get the men back to command."

"Let me tell you about these men we're after." Beidler looked at Craft scornfully. "First, one of 'em whipped a guard with his bare hands. Then the others had the brass to rescue him right under your soldier boys' noses at Rock Creek." Beidler shook his head and shoved his hand near Craft's face to prevent the young man from interrupting him. "And now, one of 'em turns out to be just about the most dangerous man with a rifle I ever saw."

"Wait a minute, Marshal," said Craft. "You said yourself he wasn't after blood when he ambushed us yesterday morning."

Ask them Sioux we fought yesterday if he's afraid to draw blood, thought Beidler. "Did you ever think the army might call you a deserter for taking off without your column?"

"They told me not to come back without that prisoner, Marshal," said Craft. "I'll send a note back with the men."

"You're a young fool."

"Maybe, but I'm coming."

"Get your gear, and don't say I didn't warn you," said Beidler. "I can't stop you from coming, but I won't wet-nurse you, and I'll leave you behind the minute you slow me down or get in my way."

Dawkins had been on the trail for at least an hour when the sun finally slipped above the hills to the east. In the growing light, he let the horse trot along the wagon trail. He hoped the boys had gotten ahead a good piece yesterday because he had a hunch somebody would be on their trail again soon.

Dawkins rode across a butte that stretched for miles to the south. Little ridges and furrows ran through the tableland, and there were many small streams born from low-lying hills covered with rocks and pines. It was good enough country to ride a horse, but a wagon would be harder to drive over and around all the rims and coulees.

Dawkins looked to his right, where Larb Creek ran north to Beaver Creek. He figured it was around thirty miles south to the murky stream's headwaters and another ten miles to the Missouri. Two hard days for a horseman, but tough to say for the wagon. He wondered if they could negotiate the badlands in the moonlight.

The country was dotted with a few prominent hills, and Dawkins thought he would climb one to check his back trail. He was not in any hurry to catch up with the Millers since they seemed to be making good time. He still thought he would find them by the end of the day. But how were they going to make the river if they were being chased?

Along about midday, Dawkins left the broad valley he was riding through and scrambled up a hill to check his back trail. He found some shade behind a boulder for the mare and climbed another fifty feet to the crest of the knob. Taking care not to skyline himself, he hid behind a large granite slab and surveyed the country to the north. He gazed for miles across the expanse of prairie and badlands, carefully examining every fold and ridge with his field glasses.

Dawkins drank from his canteen and chewed on pemmican as the heat of the early afternoon wore on him. Sweat rolled down his forehead and burned his eyes. He was thinking of leaving the hill when he spotted two riders several miles to the north. From such a distance he could not be sure if they were soldiers or Indians, but he guessed they were the men following him and the Millers. They rode well to the east of his trail, probably cutting a broad loop to avoid another ambush.

Dawkins knew it might be harder to waylay the men, all right, but it also slowed their pursuit. That gave him and the Millers more time to reach the Missouri, and they needed time if the plan Dawkins was chewing on was going to work. He watched the two horsemen awhile longer until they disappeared into a coulee. Then he climbed down to his mount and returned to the wagon trail.

Now that Dawkins had an idea of how the soldiers planned to track him, he let his horse canter at a quick pace and tried to catch up with Ezra and Jim as fast as he could.

Beidler and Craft camped along the North Fork of Beaver Creek. By the time they picketed their horses in good grass and gathered firewood, darkness had enveloped the small clearing where they laid their bedrolls. Beidler fetched water from the creek for coffee. Craft built a fire and found a green pole to spear the two prairie chickens Beidler had taken with his shotgun that day. Then he sat on a log and waited for the fire to burn down to a bed of red coals.

Beidler carried his saddlebags with him and sat across the fire from the young lieutenant. He pulled a small brown bottle from the leather bags and offered it to Craft. "Have a snort, Lieutenant?"

"Thank you, no, Marshal." Craft shook his head. "I'm a teetotaler."

"I reckon I heard of such, but hardly ever met one, least not one wearin' blue." Beidler pulled the cork and took a swig. The whiskey felt warm and good going down and made him feel more sociable. "I guess you're wondering why we peeled around to the east of those wagon tracks today."

Craft fed the fire. "I was curious about that, but I figure you know what you're doing."

Beidler took another drink, and shuddered from the bite of the liquor. "We can find that wagon track anytime we want," said Beidler. "We're not doggin' their trail in case that sharpshooter decides to ambush us again."

"How many of them do you think there are?"

"Three."

"How do you figure?"

"Before they ambushed us above the Milk, I counted two sets of horse tracks and that wagon." Beidler took a smaller drink and returned the bottle to his saddlebag. "I suppose there could be a second man riding in that wagon, but I'm guessing not. That makes three men we're after."

"It's bad enough we're outnumbered, but we have to worry about Indians, too," said Craft.

"That comes with the job, Lieutenant, especially in this country." Beidler belched and chuckled. "Hell, I've been fighting Indians for years. Killed a passel of 'em, too."

"If you don't mind my asking, Marshal, how many Indians have you killed?"

"More than I can remember, but I can tell you about the first one. I remember that one."

Craft impaled the hens on the sharpened stick and planted one end in the ground. He adjusted the height of the birds over the coals and wedged a rock under the pole to hold the weight. Then he returned his attention to Beidler. "What happened, Marshal?"

Beidler sat forward and watched the birds begin to brown. He was hungry and a little drunk. But he still felt like talking. "I was down in Colorado, running a pack train and prospecting for gold, too." He pulled his bottle out and took another drink. "Me and some fellas were camped on the Taylor River, I believe it was, ah, '60 or '61. Anyways, one evening this starvin' Comanche comes into camp beggin' for a meal. He was harmless enough, and we shared our meal with him and let 'im sleep next to the fire."

Craft turned the spit, and Beidler smelled the birds cooking. "Next morning we gave him breakfast and sent him on his way. I told him not to come back to our camp, though." Beidler edged a bit closer to the fire to chase the evening chill. "One thing about Indians, Lieutenant, they're like hungry dogs. You feed 'em once and you can't get rid of 'em. And sometimes they bring their friends with them, too."

Craft pulled the steaming pot from the fire and made coffee. "What happened then?"

"This ol' buck came back for supper the next night," said Beidler. "Found us even though we'd moved camp about fifteen miles. Well, sir, I fed him again and put 'im up for the night. Gave him breakfast too, and even sent him off with a good lunch. But I told him not to come back."

"That seems reasonable and pretty generous of you, Marshal."

"I thought so too, but damned if that buck didn't follow us again another fifteen, twenty miles and come back to our next camp." Beidler watched the birds sizzle and drip into the fire.

"What'd you do about him?"

"Killed him," said Beidler. He stirred the coals with a stick to warm them up. "I couldn't risk a gunshot. Didn't know if any of his friends were about, so I bashed his head in with a shovel. Killed his horse, too, and we buried them both the next day to hide 'em from any other Indians."

"You buried both of them?" Craft's eyes widened. "That must have taken a lot of digging."

"You're right about that. We worked like dogs, we did," said Beidler. "Not only that, but we dug a second hole, too, for dirt to hide the grave. We figured the Indians took the second pit for a prospect hole."

"Did that work? Did it throw them off?"

"Slicker'n deer guts on a door knob," said Beidler. "Them chickens need turning again, Lieutenant."

Craft rotated the spit, and the breasts of the birds were cooking to a golden brown. He sat back on the log and nodded toward Beidler. "Marshal, how did you get in this line of work?"

"I came up here from Colorado in the spring, '63 I believe it was. Started off prospecting Alder Gulch, along with every other tomfool in Beaverhead County. It didn't take long to figure out the territory needed law. It also didn't take long to figure I weren't much of a miner. Anyways, I abandoned my claim and turned to packin' freight."

Craft pulled the chickens from the fire and cut the spit in two. He handed Beidler one of the birds on the end of a stick. "You gave up prospecting after coming all the way up here from Colorado?"

"I didn't give it up entirely," said Beidler. He took the chicken from Craft and tore off a leg and a thigh. "I decided to quit prospecting for gold and prospect for human fiends instead."

Dawkins sensed the boys in the fading evening light before he saw them. He had alternately trotted and cantered his horse for several hours and figured he must be getting close to the wagon. They had rode mighty hard since they split up the day before, he thought, to have gone so far.

When Dawkins found horse dung so fresh it still steamed in the chilly evening air, he slowed to a walk and guessed where

Jim and Ezra might have stopped for the night. Up ahead a quarter of a mile, a likely looking patch of Ponderosa pine lay near a small stream. Dawkins trotted ahead and hollered when he reached the trees, "Hello, the camp! Anybody there?"

"Get your tail up here, you old man!"

Dawkins recognized Jim's voice and rode ahead until he nearly ran into the wagon around a bend in the trail.

Jim and Ezra hurried up to greet Dawkins, who dismounted and shook their hands. "Good grief. You two must have ridden all night to get this far south!"

"That's for sure." Jim laughed and pointed his thumb at Ezra. "This crazy fool kept us movin' 'til dang near midnight."

"I figured you did some night ridin' to get this far."

"How 'bout that fight you had with the soldiers?" Ezra asked. "It sounded like a regular battle."

Before Dawkins could answer, Jim blurted, "Yeah, we heard it. Sounded like a lot of shootin.'" He pointed toward Ezra. "He wanted to turn around and join the fight!"

"I'm glad you didn't," said Dawkins. "It worked out all right. Slowed 'em down for a day or so." Dawkins tied his horse to the wagon. "The real fight was that evening, against the Sioux."

"Sioux?" Jim looked at Ezra, then Dawkins. "You're pullin' my leg!"

Dawkins stretched his arms and then looked toward his back trail. "I'll tell you all about it, but first, I believe it'd be safe to build a fire and make a good meal this evening."

"You figure?" Ezra chuckled.

It was good to see Ezra smile. "Oh, they're comin' after us." Dawkins pointed to the north. "But that ambush slowed 'em down. Let's set up camp and make a meal. I'm still pickin' seeds out of my teeth from that pemmican, Ezra."

The boys laughed and returned to the wagon to unhitch the horses while Dawkins unsaddled Ezra's mare and led her to the stream. A warm meal and a decent night's sleep would be good, but he still felt the law hot on their trail. How to buy enough time to reach the Missouri and escape on a steamer?

Chapter Five

Beidler rode into the abandoned campsite and dismounted. He handed his reins to Craft and walked to the fire pit, kicking at the ashes. "They've been gone awhile, several hours, I'd say." Beidler looked back at the wagon tracks heading south. "They're only two or three days away from the Missouri, then they'll be trapped."

Craft stood in his stirrups and looked south. "If you don't mind me asking, Marshal, what's your plan?"

"We're just gonna stay behind 'em a ways," said Beidler. "When they make the river, they'll have to leave the high ground, and we'll have the advantage."

"How so?"

"I'm still not sure what they're up to, but I'm guessin' they'll either head west before they reach the river, or maybe even try to cross it." Beidler took his reins from Craft and mounted up. "That Missouri is big and wide where we're headed. I don't know how they'd manage to ford it with that ol' wagon they got. From the trail they're makin', it looks to be loaded pretty heavy, too." Beidler looked up at the afternoon sun and the stark blue sky. "At any rate, we're just giving 'em enough rope to hang themselves with. When they get off this plateau, we'll have the advantage and cut 'em off. Maybe even set up our own little ambush."

"So you think we can apprehend them?" asked Craft. "The general would sure like to see them tried, especially the one that attacked our man at Rock Creek."

"There's not a doubt in my mind that we'll catch 'em," said Beidler. "Bringing 'em in alive to stand trial is another matter, though."

"My orders are to return these men to the proper civilian authorities, where they'll stand trial," said Craft stiffly. "These men haven't been convicted yet of any crimes in a court of law." Craft removed his hat and wiped his brow.

"Lieutenant, those orders sound like they were given by someone who never gave chase to any outlaws," Beidler chuckled. "You really think we're gonna catch these men without a fight? Besides that, let's get one thing straight. I am the proper civilian authority, as you say." He opened his vest and pointed to his badge.

"Well, I suppose if they're wounded or killed in a fight while resisting arrest, that's one thing." Craft stopped and shook his head.

"Oh, don't worry, Lieutenant." The smile disappeared from Beidler's face and he walked his horse close to Craft's mount and looked the young man in the eye. "They'll get better treatment than that private at Rock Creek. They'll get a fair trial, and if they're to be hung, I'll even see to it they get a preacher to comfort their poor, miserable souls."

Dawkins had hung back a mile behind the wagon ever since they broke camp before sunrise and headed south. He kept an eye out to make sure the men following them were not drawing too near. He took advantage of every high point along the way, but so far he had been unable to spot any riders.

Not having ridden through these hills before, Dawkins was not sure how far to the south the Missouri ran. They traveled hard, from dawn until after dark, for the better part of three days, and Dawkins estimated they would reach the river in another couple of days.

He was glad to be getting close to the Missouri, but he knew that meant the men chasing them would soon press harder. Once they hit the river, it could take some time to hail a steamer, too. Scores of boats worked the Upper Missouri when he had come up the river himself in '64, but now?

Dawkins tried to stop worrying and urged his horse to a trot. He left the trail for a rocky rise to the east that looked to provide the best vantage point in the area. A short ride brought him to the base of the hill, and he rode up as far as he dared push his mount. He tied the mare to a small pine, grabbed his rifle and field glasses, and climbed another hundred yards to the crest.

The top of the hill was rounded and strewn with scrub trees and boulders, so Dawkins did not have to worry about skylining himself. He found a good spot to sit on the north-facing slope where he glassed the golden sea of rolling hills before him.

This time it did not take long for Dawkins to find his pursuers. Two horsemen rode only a few hundred yards off the wagon trail, and they were close, no farther than two miles from Dawkins's hide and another five or six from the Millers. They could catch up with the wagon in an hour or two of hard riding. Dawkins sipped from his canteen and watched the men ride closer to the trail. He was about to return to his horse when the two riders stopped at a small stream near the trail and dismounted.

Dawkins glanced to the west and guessed there must be at least two hours of good tracking light left, so he was surprised to see the men halt. He watched awhile longer and saw the riders, now within a couple of miles of the hill, making camp. They unsaddled their horses and led them down to the stream to water.

Dawkins watched the men until dusk. While he spied on them, he studied the area near the trail where they camped. He noted a single scraggly pine between their camp and where the wagon tracks ran. He also noted the small creek that passed by their camp before crossing the trail, two hundred yards to the west. Then Dawkins slipped off the hillside and returned to his horse in the growing darkness. He found the trail left by the wagon and rode as hard as he dared to find Jim and Ezra.

Beidler eyed the tall hill to the south of camp suspiciously and dropped an armload of wood next to the growing fire. He watched Craft work on supper and fetched his saddlebags and bedroll. He found his battered coffeepot and filled it from the stream. Walking back to camp, he continued to watch the wooded hillside, a mile away. He placed the pot on a flat rock along the edge of the fire and took a seat on a dead log they had dragged into camp.

"Marshal, you never told me why we stopped so early this evening," Craft said. He knelt next to the campfire and fried army-issue porkbelly in a small, cast-iron pan. "We must have had at least another two hours of light left when we stopped. It felt like we were getting near."

"Too near, I'm thinkin'," replied Beidler.

"How so?"

"We didn't loop far enough off the trail today," Beidler said. "I got impatient, too, Lieutenant. We don't want to run into another ambush, though. I thought it'd be better if we take off again early, before first light."

"Sounds good to me, Marshal." Craft turned the meat with a fork. "I guess we'll have to settle for fatback and hardtack, tonight. I'll brown the crackers in this grease here."

"I've eaten a lot worse on the trail, Lieutenant," said Beidler. He stood and stretched. "Hold down the fort, I'm going to go talk to a man about a horse."

Craft grinned and kept cooking the meat.

Beidler only saw a dim outline of the tall hill to the north in the darkness as he walked away from camp. But earlier in the day, he had seen the unmistakable glint of light reflect off some shiny object near the crest of the rock- and pine-covered rise. Someone spying on them from up there had been careless enough to reveal himself.

Now that they were getting close to the Missouri, Beidler had been turning one question over and over in his mind all day. How did these men figure to lose the law after them, once and for all? They knew they were being followed, and sooner or later, they would be caught. Beidler put himself in their shoes and tried to figure what to do if he were in the same fix. When he had seen the man spying on them from the hill, the answer had come to Beidler. They were going to try to take the offensive and steal their horses, or maybe even dry-gulch them in camp if they were desperate enough.

He decided not to share this information with that shavetail, Craft, who might give things away by not acting naturally. Besides, Beidler needed bait. And that generally worked best when the decoy did not know it was being watched.

JIM SATTERFIELD

Dawkins caught up with Jim and Ezra after dark. The boys were parked along a small stand of pines that looked like a good campsite, and they sat together on the wagon bench. Dawkins dismounted and tied his horse to the wagon. He stretched his arms and rubbed his stiff thighs.

"You ol' man," Jim said with a smile. "Want me to take care of your horse? You look whipped."

"Don't bother," said Dawkins. "I reckon you ought to leave yours saddled, too, Ezra."

Dawkins waited for both men to climb off the wagon so he could see their faces. "We got some night work to do." When both brothers remained silent, he went on. "The same two riders been followin' us are camped yonder," Dawkins pointed north, "not more'n two or three miles away."

"You sure about that, Bill?" asked Jim.

"You bet I'm sure," said Dawkins. "I watched 'em make camp and cook supper from that tall butte along the trail." He paused and added, "Watched for a couple of hours and made a map in my mind of their camp, too."

"Well now," said Jim. "Whatcha got in mind?"

Dawkins took a deep breath and exhaled slowly. He shook his head and looked at the two brothers. "We're getting close to the river, maybe two days away. Those two are playin' their cards pretty clever, just hanging back and doggin' us. They know we can't lose 'em, not with this wagon." Dawkins paused and looked up at the black sky. "We need to slip in their camp and steal their horses. That'll gain us another four or five days on 'em."

Before Dawkins could finish, Ezra blurted, "I'm no dang horse thief, Bill!"

"Neither am I, Ezra," Dawkins said patiently. "Shoot, I ain't stealing 'em for money. I don't aim to keep 'em. I figured we could picket their horses wherever we hit the river."

"I don't know about this, Bill," said Ezra. He whistled low and shook his head. "Horse thief?"

Jim laughed. "Ezra, the law already wants you for beatin' that soldier, and I'm guessin' you killed him by the way they're chasin' us." Then Jim looked at Dawkins. "They want you and me, too, for stealin' their prisoner."

"So?" asked Ezra.

"So what difference does stealin' two horses make?"

"Listen, boys," interrupted Dawkins. "I hate to take their horses, but I ain't got any plan for getting away from them two if we don't."

"Bill, how far you reckon we are from the Missouri?" asked Jim.

"Twenty miles, give or take," said Dawkins. "We'll be there in a couple of days, and them two," Dawkins paused, and pointed to the north, "will have a good long walk. With a little luck, we'll be ridin' on a steamer by the time they fetch their mounts."

Beidler sat near the fire and drank more coffee while Craft snored loudly in his bed. A sliver of a moon rose to the east, and Beidler pulled his pocket watch and noted the time. He planned to leave the campsite shortly and take a stand at the base of a lone pine from where he could watch the camp and the wagon trail leading to the south. It might cost him a good night's sleep, but he had a hunch and he was going to play it.

He had been a lawman of some sort for over twenty years. He was proud of his service to the public. Many times it had been a thankless job, and dangerous, too. He was still kicking because he had a lawman's instincts and he was not afraid to kill a man who might do him harm. Like these three they were chasing now. Maybe one of them had risked his neck to guard the soldiers' flank against the Sioux, but they were still outlaws, and it was his duty to bring them in. The judge could sort out the particulars.

Beidler fed the fire once more and finished his coffee. He ambled over to his saddle, next to Craft lying in his blanket, and fetched a blanket and his shotgun. Then he quietly walked to a lone pine between camp and the wagon trail. With his blanket draped over his shoulders, Beidler sat against the tree, waiting and looking into darkness.

Chapter Six

Dawkins and the Millers had been riding for an hour when they came to the tall butte to their right. It rose from the prairie like a dark wall. Only a quarter of a moon shone overhead, and the stars twinkled brightly now that they had awakened in the heart of the night. Dawkins raised his arm and motioned for Jim and Ezra to come up and talk. "We're close now," Dawkins whispered. He shielded a match and looked at his watch. "Their camp is another mile or so north. We'll ride a bit longer, then we'll walk."

"Think you can find their camp?" asked Jim, low and soft. "It's awful dark tonight."

"I reckon so." Dawkins looked ahead and then back to the Millers. He smiled to ease their fears. "Just follow me. I can see this wagon trail good enough."

"Bill," Ezra whispered, "how much time we got?"

"It's just past midnight," answered Dawkins. "We got plenty of time. No need to rush." Almost as an afterthought, he added, "No more talkin'."

Dawkins took the lead again, and they rode single file into the dark. He gauged their progress against the map in his mind, etched deeply from two hours of study from the tall butte. He hoped they could slip into that camp and steal those horses without a fight. He would leave Ezra with their mounts, maybe a quarter of a mile from the camp, and take Jim with him. The two of them had rescued Ezra from the soldiers' camp slick as a whistle. They worked well together at night.

Dawkins rode on, rocking and swaying to the gait of his mount. The only sounds were from the clicking of the horses' hooves on the gravel and rock along the trail. Funny thing about night riding, he thought, there was no one at all to share your thoughts with, or even your fears. There was nothing to see or distract a man from all the possibilities. At least the dark sharpened his senses, though, and he rode on, running the lay of the land through his mind and how he might approach the camp.

When they reached a low ridge, Dawkins stopped and waited for Jim and Ezra to come up. Dawkins dismounted and motioned for the Millers to follow suit. He pressed a finger to his lips, handed Ezra his reins, and motioned for Jim to do the same. Then Dawkins and Jim slowly walked to the top of the swale.

When they reached the ridgeline, Dawkins looked to the north and soon spotted a dim campfire in the distance. He nudged Jim and pointed toward the camp. Jim nodded, and Dawkins studied the rolling prairie between them and the camp. The fire looked to be at least a half mile away, and several small knolls dotted the way. Chest-high sagebrush provided more cover, and a northerly breeze seemed like a good omen. He looked toward the campfire a little longer and then nodded back toward Ezra.

Dawkins and Jim returned to Ezra, and the three men huddled close together. "Camp's about a thousand yards north," whispered Dawkins hoarsely. "Far enough away, they shouldn't hear our horses neighin', but try to keep 'em quiet just the same."

THE RIVER'S SONG

"You sure about me stayin' here, Bill?" asked Ezra in a loud whisper.

Dawkins motioned with his hand for him to be quieter. "Need you to keep the horses." He looked at Jim and then back to Ezra. "We might be needing 'em in a hurry, but don't be leaving this spot, no matter what you hear. Just wait for us."

Ezra nodded, and Dawkins looked at Jim. "Let's go, hoss."

They walked back to the low ridge and headed toward the camp. Dawkins watched his step and tried not to scrape the sagebrush, but he made good time for a half a mile. He wanted to reach a knoll that looked to be within a couple hundred yards of the camp. The fire grew dimmer, but Dawkins still saw it every time they came to a high spot on the prairie.

Soon Dawkins and Jim reached the base of the knoll, and they both scurried to the top. The camp was closer than Dawkins had figured, no more than a hundred yards away. He leaned over to Jim and whispered in his ear, "We're gonna wait here awhile, look things over."

Dawkins could not see anyone moving about the fire and figured the men were bedded down for the night. He saw where the stream ran beyond the camp, just a trickle of a creek, and he noted the lone pine tree, perhaps fifty yards from the fire. He looked closer into the darkness, trying to spot their horses.

Jim poked him with his elbow and whispered, "I see their horses. Must be a picket line runnin' off that tree. See 'em?"

Dawkins nodded and they headed toward the horses. Nearing the pine where the picket line was tied, Dawkins and Jim passed close to the fire, no more than twenty yards to their right. Dawkins hid behind sagebrush and peered into the camp. The fire was only a red and gray bed of coals, no longer casting much light. He looked hard for sleeping men and motioned for Jim to look as well. After a moment, Jim pointed to the right of the fire and then held up one finger. Dawkins saw the blanketed lump on the ground, but it bothered him not to see a second.

They moved on around the camp and nearer to the tree, which was only a stone's throw away. When they came to within twenty or thirty yards of the pine, the sagebrush petered out, leaving no cover to conceal them. Dawkins studied the horses picketed to a rope running off the far side of the tree. He almost gasped from surprise and fear when he saw the silhouette of a man sitting against the tree, looking north. Dawkins crouched lower behind the last of the sagebrush and pointed toward the man to warn Jim. He saw Jim's eyes widen and knew he had spotted the man as well. Dawkins pointed at Jim, and then back at the campfire. Jim turned and retreated toward the sleeping man near the fire while Dawkins watched the man sitting at the base of the tree and planned a stalk.

Beidler's eyes grew heavy now that the coffee had worn off. His blanket kept him warm on the cool prairie night and he might have slept, but he needed to make water. He figured now was the time to relieve himself. It was not that late, and he could settle back down against the tree until dawn. He had not heard a thing since he took his post, but the night was young and he did not expect any visitors until much later.

He rose from the tree and took a few steps into the darkness. It felt good to get rid of all that coffee and stretch for a few moments. When he returned to the tree, he was shocked to see a tall figure step from behind the trunk and aim a pistol at his head.

Beidler heard the four distinctive clicks of a Colt army revolver being cocked and then a liquid voice, "Drop that shotgun, now." The man stepped closer and stuck the pistol in his face. "Drop the shotgun, now…I won't ask again."

Beidler recovered his wits and caught his breath. He bent over a little at the waist and extended his arms, and the gun fell to the ground, making a dull thud.

The stranger kept the pistol near his face and said, "Left hand, drop your gun belt."

Beidler hoped the outlaw would not think about a pistol under the blanket that was still draped over his shoulders. He considered going for his revolver but did not think he would make it with that cocked Colt pointing less than a foot from his face. He unbuckled his belt with his left hand, and his holster dropped to the ground.

"Now back up and sit down against that tree."

When Beidler complied, the man took a knee and pulled the shotgun and the gunbelt away from the tall pine. Then he whistled low and stood up again, all the while keeping the pistol trained on Beidler's head.

Beidler recovered from the shock of being held up, and brief fear turned to seething anger. He clenched his fists, and his neck tightened. This outlaw had come into his camp and disarmed him. He would chase this outlaw to the end of the earth. His anger turned to shock once more when another figure materialized out of the dark and approached the first man with the Colt. The second outlaw spoke, "Don't worry about that other one." He nodded toward the fire. "You can hear him snoring from here."

"Untie them two horses," the first man ordered. "And bring 'em around."

The leader jerked his head when Beidler spoke for the first time. "I wouldn't have taken you for a horse thief."

"I'm gonna set you afoot, all right, but we ain't horse thieves."

"Yes, by God, I think you are, by the way you have acted."

The second man mounted one horse bareback and led the second by the halter. He rode up a few yards behind the leader. "Let's git."

The leader kept his pistol pointed at Beidler while he handed the shotgun and gunbelt to the mounted outlaw. "You'll find these just a ways out on the prairie come first light." He took the lead rope of the second horse and holstered his pistol. "Look for your horses at the end of the wagon tracks, somewhere along the river." The man grabbed the horse's mane and leaped onto its back. Then the two men bolted off into the dark.

Chapter Seven

Captain Joseph La Barge stood in the pilothouse of the *John M. Chambers*, steering the steamer up the treacherous Missouri. He had moored earlier in the day at the Fort Peck landing to take on firewood and sweet water for his passengers. Now the veteran pilot navigated past the confluence of the Milk and Missouri, where snags and hidden sandbars had wrecked many a boat in the blink of an eye.

La Barge had spent more of his sixty-four years on a boat than on dry land. For nearly fifty years, he explored the Missouri, first in the fur trade, and for the last twenty as a contractor to the federal government, US Army, and various private interests wishing to freight goods upriver. This would be La Barge's last commercial trip to Fort Benton. Upon his return to St. Louis, he planned to sell the *Chambers* and spend his remaining years in retirement with his wife, Pelagie.

Passing the Milk, La Barge noted the tributary ran low for late July. He knew the heavy summer rains had abated. He had heard that wet weather had plagued General Miles earlier in July during his chase of Sitting Bull, but over the last two weeks, the country had dried up. After the Milk, the Missouri constricted noticeably, and La Barge hoped for an easy trip without too many sandbar crossings.

The Missouri was his home, and he might never again see the upper reaches. The last leg of the trip, from Fort Peck to Fort Benton, was his favorite stretch of the mighty river. But he was already worried about problems with his fuel and food supplies.

La Barge had obtained only green cottonwood and a few drift logs from Fort Peck. He would exhaust his supply of rosin keeping the wet wood making steam. He needed to find pine or dried cottonwood, but he was still at least two days from the Breaks country where the best wood was found.

Then there was the meat supply. The recent troubles with the Sioux had spooked his hunters, and two men left his employ at Fort Peck. They warned La Barge they would not venture from the boat once they reached the Milk. The old captain called their bluff and told them to make meat or leave the boat. So they left.

The ship stores held enough salt pork, lyed corn, and navy beans to feed the crew. But the more distinguished passengers, men and women of wealth and accomplishment, expected better cuisine. On the upper reach of the river, wild game, expertly prepared by the kitchen, was the normal bill of fare. But that required hunters capable of harvesting buffalo, elk, deer, and antelope on a daily basis while avoiding hostile Indians.

La Barge steamed upriver, over three hundred river miles from Fort Benton, low on fuel and meat. Responsible for over two hundred souls, his boat crew consisted of the most seasoned men he had ever assembled. La Barge and the other officers stayed in a suite of rooms on the third deck, known as the texas. But the best spot on the ship, the pilothouse, belonged to one man and one man only, the captain.

When La Barge negotiated an easy stretch of river, particularly in the good light and calm wind of morning or late afternoon, he welcomed guests to the pilothouse. He enjoyed regaling passengers with his adventures from a lifetime on the river. To break the monotony of the trip, he told stories of storms, rapids, whirlpools, fires, Indian fights, and great herds of buffalo. La Barge liked people, and on every voyage he made new friends, some for life. He tolerated the stuffy, self-important wealthy and powerful. He had spent his share of time with senators, governors, and generals, and politely and dutifully entertained them. But his favorite guests were those who shared his love of nature and the beauty of the Upper Missouri.

On this voyage, one such guest was the lovely Dr. Adeline Johnston. She was the fiancée of an important Seattle merchant and was traveling cross-country from her home in Georgia to marry the man. Only she had eschewed the more traditional route of travel her fiancé had offered, a private railroad car, for the chance to steam up the Missouri River.

La Barge made her acquaintance when one of the crew broke his leg while ashore wooding the boat. It was an ugly wound, with both bones below his knee snapping and piercing the skin. The mate was in great pain, and his screams drew the attention of most of the passengers. One of La Barge's officers had some training in medicine, but Dr. Johnston brushed him aside when the wounded man was swung back to the ship on the hauling stage. None of the officers or La Barge had ever met or been a patient of a woman doctor, but she took command of the situation and treated the crewman. The man would be on crutches for some time, but his flesh wounds had healed and his broken bones were mending straight and true.

As a dinner guest that evening at the captain's table, Dr. Johnston explained she had recently graduated from the Woman's Medical College of Pennsylvania. In her teens, she had found her calling while serving in the Medical Corps of the Confederate Army. While she explained her interest and experience in medicine, La Barge and most of his officers found themselves quite distracted by her charm and beauty.

La Barge guessed she was in her early thirties. She had lustrous dark hair she wore in a tight bun and deep, brown eyes. Her skin was perfect, and she had a genuine smile. Taller than many of the officers, she had a slender figure. But most of all, she had an infectious laugh, and La Barge loved her Southern accent.

Over the last several weeks La Barge and Dr. Johnston, or Adel, as she insisted he call her, had become friends. She was one of his most frequent visitors to the pilothouse, where she spent hours taking in the aura and mystery of the river. On the last trip through his beloved Upper Missouri, Captain La Barge took great pleasure in sharing the river with someone as thoughtful and inquisitive as Adel.

Adel spent the afternoon catching up on her correspondence, one letter to George, her fiancé, and a second to the newly created First Providence Hospital in Seattle, where she was to join the staff in the fall. After a light lunch, she returned to her private room on the hurricane suite. She hurriedly dressed to join Captain La Barge in the pilothouse while the light on the river was still flat and the wind calm. She was welcome as long as the sailing conditions were good. She suspected he might allow her to remain under more difficult circumstances, but she would never take advantage of his friendship.

When the *Chambers* passed the confluence of the Milk River, Captain La Barge told her they would soon reach the most beautiful country of the voyage, where the land rose above the

THE RIVER'S SONG

banks into rock- and timber-covered cliffs and buttes. He also promised her that when they were safely past Sioux country, there were bends along the river where she could ramble across the bottomland and prairie and rejoin the boat on the other side. After weeks on the steamer, she longed for a walk and solitude, even with a guide accompanying her for protection.

Besides the grand view from the pilothouse and Captain La Barge's interesting stories, there was another reason Adel sought his company. Captain La Barge had that rarest of skills among men, she had found. He actually listened when she spoke to him. She was unsure of herself, with her decision to marry and begin a new career as a medical doctor. He was intuitive enough to sense this hesitance and had gladly considered her personal and career aspirations. So far, he had not presumed to advise her, but she suspected he was forming some definite opinions of her plans. With her parents deceased, it meant a lot to have the counsel of someone of such high standing and character.

Adel wound her dark hair into a bun at her neck. She carefully pinned her broad, straw hat into her hair and looked once more into the mirror. Leaving her room, she stepped onto the hurricane deck and walked to the stairway that led through the texas and up to the pilothouse.

La Barge stood behind the wheel of the *Chambers*, enjoying the evening run of the river. Earlier in the afternoon, a stiff headwind had pushed around the two-hundred-foot boat and created a chop and then surface waves on the river. He was compelled to make for shore and wait for better sailing conditions. La Barge tried to make use of the idleness by landing a wood-cutting party on the south shore. The men managed to augment the fuel supply with drift logs and some standing dead cottonwoods, but they still required better wood to reach Fort Benton.

Now the river was smooth and glassy, and La Barge easily spotted the snags that could swamp the boat or punch a hole in her bottom. A deckhand on the bow sounded the bottom with a long pole and sang out the depth every few seconds. Tall cottonwoods along both shores towered over the boat, and the sun was dropping below the river to the west. La Barge heard a gentle knock and smiled when he saw Adel wave.

"Welcome to my office," said La Barge, opening the pilothouse door. "You've chosen a splendid evening to visit."

"Good evening, Captain." Adel looked through the front window of the small, glass-sided quarters. "I have never seen sunsets like these on the Missouri. All the fiery reds and pale oranges, and the way they stretch nearly overhead."

"I had an artist on one of these runs," said La Barge. "He set up his easel on the deck in front of the texas. He would drink wine and paint. Some nights we had to help him back to his room." La Barge paused, and chuckled. "He never quite got the colors right. I think he was more interested in the wine than his work."

Adel laughed, and then asked, "When do you think I'll be able to leave the boat? The voyage has been wonderful, but I'd love to walk the bottomland, smell the cottonwoods, listen to the birds. Just for a little while."

"Of course, perhaps in a few days. It depends on how much river we make." La Barge paused.

"What's wrong, Captain?"

"Well, you're perfectly safe here, but I would like to put a few more miles behind this Sioux country," said La Barge. "Even the wood parties make me nervous. I've lost a lot of men over the years around the Milk River. We're generally out of their country when we reach the Musselshell."

They stood for a while in awkward silence, and La Barge suspected Adel had something troubling her. He pointed out a flock of trumpeter swans along the north bank. The setting sun painted the white fowl in a pink hue, and he said, "When this voyage is over, I shall miss this very much."

Adel nodded. "Captain, how old were you when you married Mrs. La Barge?" Her face reddened. "I hope you don't mind my asking."

"Not at all, Adel." La Barge tried to keep his eyes on the river. "We married in 1842. I was twenty-six and Pelagie was seventeen."

"How did you meet your wife?"

"I knew her and her family from childhood," said La Barge. "Both our families were from St. Louis."

La Barge saw Adel was about to speak, and then she paused and bit her lower lip. He asked, "You've never told me how you met your fiancé." He glanced her way and smiled before returning his attention to the river.

"George and I met a year ago in the summer, before my last year of instruction at medical college. Of all places, we met at Gettysburg, on the battlefield."

La Barge glanced her way with an inquisitive look.

"Some of my friends, other students, and I wanted to tour the battlefield. We took the train down from Philadelphia." She paused, "George fought at Gettysburg…for the Federals. He had traveled from Seattle to visit relatives in New York and attend a reunion of his regiment at Gettysburg. We met at a reception given by the memorial association."

"I see," said La Barge, hoping to coax Adel into telling more.

"Mr. Tailor, ah, George, is older than I am, and a widower."

La Barge knew it was bold but still asked, "What interested you in him?"

Without hesitation she said, "He supported my becoming a doctor. He had been wounded several times in battle and truly valued my work."

"That's important."

"Captain, all my life, people have told me that it is not woman's work to be a doctor." Adel's eyes watered, and she wiped them with her scarf. "I suspect I'll not be having children, medicine is my life. And I believe George will respect my choice."

"Does Mr. Tailor have children from his first marriage?" La Barge kept his eyes on the darkening river front.

"Two sons, both young men who now work in the family business, but we haven't met."

"How did this chance encounter at Gettysburg lead you to matrimony?"

"After I returned to Philadelphia, we corresponded regularly." The pilothouse was cooler, with the sun nearly gone, and Adel covered her shoulders with a shawl. "George wrote during Christmas, suggesting marriage, and I accepted." She paused and added, "Of course, he agreed to wait until after my graduation."

"Of course," added La Barge.

"I was fortunate to obtain my position at First Providence, where I can pursue my profession and live in Seattle with my husband."

"Hmm," mused La Barge. He wanted to ask a question of this charming woman but was afraid it might be forward of him.

"What, Captain?" Adel looked pleadingly into his eyes. "Please tell me, what are you thinking?"

"Do you love him, Adel?"

Adel closed her eyes and pursed her lips. "I admire him, he's a fine man. I think I will come to love him."

"I'm sure you will, my dear," said La Barge. "Unfortunately, I believe I will have to bid you adieu. We're out of light, and I need to moor the boat for the night." La Barge kept one hand on the wheel and opened the glass door for Adel with his other. "Sleep well, and perhaps we can get you off this boat in the next day or two."

"Thank you for listening, Captain."

"My pleasure."

La Barge watched Adel leave the texas and walk down the ramp to the hurricane deck. The sun had disappeared below the river, and he steered for a likely spot along the south shore, carefully watching the crewman on the bow sounding the depth. In the dusk, the river traded its muddy hue for a silver glimmer from the rising moon. Nearing shore, La Barge smelled sweet cottonwoods and heard waterfowl scold the invading boat. He hoped for Adel's happiness.

Chapter Eight

"There she is, boys." Dawkins stepped to the edge of the rim and pointed below where the canyon fell away hundreds of feet to a ribbon of mud-tinged water. "That's the Missouri."

"Good God, Bill," said Jim, shaking his head. "How are we gonna get down there?"

Dawkins looked upstream. "Come first light, we'll head down there and cut that coulee, yonder." He motioned to the west, where the sun had nearly disappeared. "Won't be any trouble t'all to make the river from there. Should be a good landing, too, where that creek joins the river."

Ezra looked behind them. "Maybe we ought to be movin' on now, with them two followin' us."

"I don't think so, hoss." Dawkins grinned and stretched. "We don't want to try crossing that kind of ground in the dark. We'll head out early, though." He nodded to the north. "Besides, we got at least a couple of days before them two get anywhere near this far."

"You reckon?" Jim asked. "They gotta be madder than hornets for getting their horses stolen. They're gonna be walkin' their tails off to catch us. I'll feel a lot safer when we're steamin' up that river."

"Me too, Jim," said Dawkins. "But we're safe for a while. Think how hard we traveled the last two days to get this far. And we're riding, with a couple of extra mounts to boot." He pointed toward the two horses they had stolen, tied to the wagon. "Not only did we leave them two on foot, but they either got to carry all their gear, or cache it and go back. I'd guess they'll be lugging it all with 'em, saddles, tack, rifles, food, everything they got."

"Can't argue with you there, Bill," said Jim. "First we traveled nearly all night after we slipped into their camp, and then we hardly stopped last night as well."

"We'll take a good rest tonight," said Dawkins. "Build a fire, cook some grub, and get on down to that river come first light."

Jim climbed into the back of the wagon and rummaged through gear and hides. In a moment he raised up, holding a jug covered in fancy Métis wickerwork. "I think we earned us a snort, what do ya say, Bill?"

"I've got a terrible dry. Take a pull and pass that demijohn along."

The men sat on the edge of the canyon and drank trade whiskey in the growing darkness. Dawkins took a second hot swig, and the liquor burned all the way down to his empty stomach. None of them had eaten much in the last two days, running from the law, and he knew he had better get some food going, but that whiskey tasted good. It loosened his tongue, and he told the boys something he was not sure he was going to share. "I know one of them men who's after us, leastwise I know who he is."

"Your pullin' my leg," Jim slurred.

"The little man, sittin' up against the tree?" Dawkins grabbed the jug from Jim and took a drink, then wiped his mouth with his sleeve. "He's a US Marshal, deputy, that is, out of Helena. Name's Beidler. But everybody knows him as X."

Ezra whistled low. "X. Beidler? Vigilante X?" He laughed drunkenly. "We stole his horse?"

"Yep." Dawkins said. "You know the man, too?"

"Heck, no, but who ain't heard of X. Beidler?"

"I don't know him either," said Dawkins. "But I recognized him right off the other night. Sawed off little son-of-a-buck with that droopy ol' mustache. Makes sense, too, him being up here. Probably tagging along with General Miles after some of Sitting Bull's outlaw Sioux."

"So we got Deputy Marshal Beidler after us now," Jim muttered. "Well, if you're gonna be a bear, be a grizzly." He laughed and looked around. "Hey, where'd that jug run off to?"

"We probably better get to tendin' these horses and makin' some grub." Dawkins rose and stood on wobbly legs. "Best remember this spot, looks like a good place to glass the river for boats." The Missouri ran to the east as far as he could see, shimmering in the moonlight. Two days, he thought, was as long as they dared wait on a boat, then they would have to leave the wagon and most of their belongings behind and head west on horseback.

"Marshal, I'm just about played out," said Lieutenant Craft. "This little creek looks like as good a spot as any to bivouac. Besides, it's so dark I can barely see where I'm going."

"I reckon it'll do, Lieutenant." Beidler dropped the saddle off his shoulder and bent at the waist, hands on his knees, to catch his breath. "It's hell bein' your own horse." He straightened and tried to stretch the knots out of his back. He was nearly fifty years old and felt every day of it after walking for two days almost nonstop since their horses had been stolen. He looked over at Craft, who had fallen to the ground in exhaustion. "Don't fall asleep just yet. We need to get a fire goin' and eat."

Craft rolled over on his back. "Marshal, we're just about out of food. What do we need a fire for?" He sat up and pointed to his saddlebags. "All we have left is hardtack and some dried meat."

"Bull," snorted Beidler. "We got this." He walked over to his saddlebag and pulled out five feet of dead rattlesnake. He had nearly stepped on it earlier in the day, walking in an exhausted daze across the prairie. He should have been paying attention and was mighty lucky to hear the snake rattle before it struck. It hit the heel of his boot, and Beidler stepped back and blew a hole through its head with his Colt. "This'll eat just fine."

"I don't know, Marshal," said Craft. "I might just stick with the hardtack."

"No sir, that's breakfast." Beidler walked to the small creek and cleaned the snake. First, he cut off what was left of its head and threw it in the brush. He also cut off the rattle and placed it in his shirt pocket. Beidler pulled off the skin like a man would take off a sock. Then he gutted it like a long, skinny fish and cut the carcass into several pieces. The meat gleamed white in the pale moonlight.

By the time Beidler was done, Craft had a fire going and filled the canteens. Beidler cut a couple of long, straight willows along the creek and returned to camp. He sat against his saddle and impaled a piece of snake on one of the sticks. "Ain't nothing to eatin' rattler, Lieutenant. Here, catch." He tossed Craft a piece of the snake and laughed at the way the greenhorn juggled it, as if it still might bite him.

Craft stuck the meat on the end of the willow and dangled it above the flames of the fire. "Think we'll ever catch up with those men on foot, Marshal?"

"We'll just keep followin' that damned wagon," said Beidler. "So far, they're headin' straight for the river."

"Think they'll really leave our horses where we can find them?"

"They might, if they catch a boat like they're plannin'," said Beidler. He eyed his snake, which was nearly cooked. "See, I figured it out. Don't know why it didn't come to me sooner, but they're hopin' to hail a steamer." He took his meat from the fire and blew on it some. "Trick to eatin' snake is to get all the meat between the ribs and along the back." Beidler ate for a while and then spoke with his mouth full of rattlesnake. "Looks like yours is done, Lieutenant. Don't want to cook it too much, lose all the flavor."

Craft's nose wrinkled as he looked at his piece of snake, yellowish now from the fire. He nibbled carefully along the backbone and gagged a little, but kept eating and washed it down with a long drink from his canteen.

"Good, ain't it?" said Beidler. He tossed another piece of raw snake across the fire into Craft's lap. "Have another. Waste not, want not."

Craft impaled the meat on his stick. "If we're just following their trail to fetch our horses, why are we pushing so hard, Marshal?"

"'Cause it ain't certain there'll be a boat," said Beidler. "The sooner we catch up with 'em, the less time they'll have to get a ride. I figure we'll reach the river within a couple of days."

"Marshal," asked Craft, "have you ever had your horse stolen before?"

Beidler stopped chewing. Anger welled within him. His jaws tightened and he stirred the fire with his willow stick.

"Back in '63, when I was in Virginia City, there was a fellow who stole my ol' mule, Black Bess. Son-of-a-buck had the brass to return her to me, a week later, all worn out and lame. Said he had just borrowed her."

Craft threw the last bit of his snake in the fire. "What'd you do?"

"I told him if I ever caught him on an animal of mine again, I'd kill him."

Craft chuckled. "I bet he never borrowed a horse of yours again."

"Nope," said Beidler, "but I helped hang him all the same. The man's name was Ives, and horse stealin' was the least of his crimes." Beidler untied the bedroll from his saddle and unrolled it on the ground. "These fellows we're after signed their own death warrants, too, when they left us afoot in wild country like this. I don't care if they do leave our horses for us."

Dawkins fed the fire and looked over to where Jim and Ezra lay. The twins snored in harmony, half drunk and exhausted. The night was clear, and they had not fooled with a tent or a lean-to. Dawkins wanted to be off early in the morning, so they roasted venison on the fire and made pan bread, enough for supper and breakfast. Drinking the last of his coffee, he looked past the edge of the canyon to the Missouri River, downstream to the east. Sure better be a steamer headed this way.

Dawkins looked over to the twins and chuckled. Couple of pups, he thought. Not a care in the world, why worry about tomorrow? Well, maybe Ezra had learned some about how hard life could be, losing Belle to a soldier's poor aim. But he looked to be getting past it.

JIM SATTERFIELD

Bill Dawkins, you've seen forty winters. Everything you own is in that wagon. Getting too old to run like this. No prospects, no wealth, no wife. Where the hell did life go? Seems like just yesterday you got your discharge and you thought you were the luckiest man in Pennsylvania to get out of that war in one piece. Took a steamer to the territory, figured you'd strike it rich. You and a thousand other fools. Won't give up though, never give up. Maybe it would all mean something if you could look after them boys, see them through this mess, help them get a new start.

Chapter Nine

Dawkins worked the wagon down the grassy coulee, a half mile from the north bank of the Missouri. Low-hanging patches of fog the old mountain men called witches' breath drifted along the side of the deep canyon. The sun had barely cleared the horizon when Ezra rode back to the wagon. Dawkins figured Ezra was coming to lead him through the last strip of timber running down to the river. But the lad was grinning and pointed toward the pines.

"Bill, Bill," Ezra spoke in loud whisper, "I left Jim down there in the woods. There's a herd of elk workin' across the hill below us."

"How far away?"

Ezra turned in his saddle and looked down the coulee. "Not far. Couple o' hundred yards."

Dawkins nodded and pulled the wagon brake. He reached behind the bench and found his Sharps and an ammunition belt. "Tie your horse to the wagon and find a couple of rocks to block the wheels." Dawkins gathered his gear and jumped off the bench. He inspected the parked wagon and then winked at Ezra. "Let's go make some meat."

The two men walked swiftly down the coulee until they came to the edge of a thin stand of pines. The pitch of the land steepened, and they hid behind the trees to spot Jim. After a few moments Ezra whispered, "There he is, right in front of us, maybe fifty yards."

Dawkins peered beyond Jim, but could not see the elk. It looked as if there was a draw beyond Jim's position, so they scurried toward him. As they drew near, they leaned over and Dawkins tapped Jim's shoulder. "Whatcha got?"

Jim pointed below to a small clearing, and Dawkins saw a string of cow elk emerge from the trees, moving to the right. In a minute or two, the herd would be directly in front of them, no more than a hundred yards away. Dawkins motioned for Jim and Ezra to huddle near. "I'll shoot the lead cow, then you two let'em have it. Spread out and get the rest."

Dawkins loaded the Sharps and knelt against a tall pine. The herd had made its way into the small meadow, and Dawkins noticed a big bull, with velvet-covered antlers, bringing up the rear. He turned his attention to the first cow, still walking and testing the wind. She acted spooky, glancing about and stomping her front hooves. Dawkins thought their scent might have reached the elk. He cocked his rifle and peered through his sights. When he whistled, the cow stopped in mid-step and looked up the hill. Dawkins steadied the sights on her shoulder and squeezed the trigger.

A heartbeat after his shot, Jim and Ezra fired. Dawkins's cow fell. Another cow collapsed before reaching the timber, and a spike wobbled and looked to drop any moment. Most of the herd stilled milled about in the clearing, unable to determine the source of the gunfire. Dawkins whispered, "Both of you, shoot one more." He watched as two more elk, a cow and a young bull, fell to Jim and Ezra's rifles. Dawkins stood and hollered, "That's good, that's enough butcherin' for one day." The rest of the herd jerked their heads toward the men, then ran across the clearing and disappeared into the pines.

"Boys, that's our first payment on a boat ride upriver." Dawkins looked over to Jim. "Why don't you get on down there and start gutting those elk. Me and Ezra will fetch the wagon and join you directly."

"Five elk's not bad, but we could have got more, Bill," said Jim.

"Yeah, but it's gonna be another hot one." Dawkins looked up at a clear blue sky and already felt the sun clearing the eastern skyline. "We need to gut these animals and skin 'em. We'll hang 'em in the timber near the river when we're done."

Running into the elk herd so close to the river was a good piece of luck, Dawkins thought as he walked back to the wagon. Now they needed to find a suitable spot along the shore where a boat could moor and swing out a landing stage. Just had to hurry up and wait.

Dawkins and the Millers reached the riverbank in early afternoon. After skinning buffalo all summer, the men were well practiced in butchering game and quickly cleaned the five elk. The carcasses cooled in the shade of the last timber stretching down near the shoreline. The men dismounted and walked to the edge of the Missouri, staring upstream, hoping to spot a boat.

Willows and a few sparse cottonwoods lined the bank. Ezra read Dawkins's mind, "Can't see nearly as well downriver as we could from our camp along the ridge last night."

Dawkins nodded but studied the bank, silently judging the depth of the river and looking for snags or sandbars that would block a boat. "I noticed last night the main channel runs along the north shore, here." He nodded and rubbed his chin. "That's good. Any boat traffic will be coming along this side of the river. That far bank must be two or three hundred yards away. It would be hard to raise a boat from that distance."

"Bill, what the heck do we do now?" asked Jim.

Dawkins glanced behind them, back toward the stringer of pines running down to the river. "That's some good fuel for a steamboat." Dawkins pointed to the pines. "Let's take care of our stock, get 'em watered and picket them in good grass. Then we ought to get our axes and start cutting any standing dead logs in that stand yonder."

"Bill, you figure we'll just camp along the river?" asked Jim.

"Might as well, stay ready for a boat. I don't see any reason why a good pilot couldn't land along this here shoreline. Even a fully loaded ship will only draw four or five feet." Dawkins took a deep breath and sighed. "Anyways, I'll help get things going here with the stock and wood cuttin', but later I'm gonna ride back up with my field glasses to our campsite from last night. See if I can't spot us a boat."

The men worked through the afternoon, downing dead trees above the river. They trimmed the branches and used one of the horses they kept in a harness to drag the logs down to the shoreline. By the time the sun was an hour or two above the river to the west, they had a pile of logs taller than a man could see over.

"Boys, this is a good start. I'm going to take off for the ridgeline." Dawkins pointed behind them. "Now that the wind has calmed down and the water's getting' glassy, any boats about ought to be movin'." He fetched his rifle and field glasses from the wagon and saddled one of the horses. Dawkins left Jim and Ezra cutting timber and rode near on his way up the coulee to the ridge. "I'll be back a little after dark. You boys knock off after a bit and get some grub going."

Jim rested his ax and grinned. "How 'bout some fresh elk liver?"

"That'd be fine," said Dawkins. "I like mine with taters and gravy."

"Maybe you want buttermilk and cobbler, too?" asked Jim.

Ezra snickered and Dawkins waved, then nudged his horse and trotted up the slope to the ridge.

The ride back to the top of the canyon without the wagon did not take long, and Dawkins reached the rim with daylight to spare. He rode along the wagon track until he reached their camp from the night before and dismounted. He tied his horse to a scrubby pine and removed his field glasses from the leather case looped over the saddle horn. Walking to the edge of the rim, he sat down to study the river.

Right off, Dawkins gasped at the sight of an enormous steamship, riding high above the water, no more than a mile downstream. With trembling hands, he raised his field glasses to examine the ship more carefully. He judged it to be a big boat, at least two hundred feet. Counting the pilothouse, it had four decks and was painted solid white. With all the windows glittering in the evening sun, the steamer looked like a floating palace. The stern wheel churned the river into froth, and two black chimneys towering above the pilothouse left parallel trails of smoke that merged well behind the boat.

Dawkins lowered his field glasses and looked for a route down to the river, where he could hale the steamer. He noticed the boat was veering from the far bank to his side, to follow the main channel. He mounted his horse and rode along the steep ridge to the east for a few hundred yards before the slope lessened and he was able to ride at an oblique toward the steamer.

Once he dropped off the ridgeline, Dawkins only saw the boat intermittently, through the pines and junipers. He spotted smoke above the timber, though, and the steamer was still well downstream of the tall cottonwood he aimed to reach. When he came to the foot of the ridge, his view of the river was blocked. He headed for the shore, savoring the dark coolness and sweet scent of the bottomland. It smelled of willows and cottonwoods, wildflowers and freedom. Soon he saw patches of brown, slick water between the trees bordering the Missouri, and then he was standing on the bank with a steamship headed right toward him, not a quarter of a mile away.

"Captain, I see what you mean about the upper river," said Adel. "It's getting much more rugged and steep as we head west."

"Notice, too, the pines and cedars now along the hills," said La Barge as he steered the *Chambers* up a straight stretch of river, glassy in the evening calm. "This rough country; the local folk call it the Missouri Breaks. Soon the canyons will be even deeper—"

"Captain, I beg your pardon," interrupted Adel, "but what's that along the north shore?" She pointed a few hundred yards upriver.

La Barge scanned the shoreline ahead of the steamer and spotted something white fluttering along the shore. He raised his field glasses. "There's a man waving some sort of flag on the bank, Adel." He lowered his glasses. "We'll slow down and see if we can make our way to him. Otherwise we'll have to send the yawl."

La Barge signaled twice with the ship's whistle, then called a young mate to the pilothouse. The captain pointed toward the man, who kept waving a white cloth furled to a tree limb, and ordered, "Go to the bow and let me know what he has to say."

La Barge hoped the channel was deep enough to steam near the shore. A deckhand sounded the bottom with a long pole from the bow. He slowed the boat to a near standstill, and soon they were alongside the stranger. The mate spoke to the man and then hurried back to the pilothouse.

Adel opened the door, and the mate entered and motioned toward the stranger walking along the shore. "Captain, that man wants to speak with you or one of the officers about gaining passage on the *Chambers* to Fort Benton."

"What did he have to say?" asked La Barge.

"He says there are two other men in his party, located a mile or so upstream on this shore. He says they have a good supply of fuel for us and fresh meat, lots of it, sir."

"Are they near a good landing?"

"Yes sir, he mentioned that he thought we'd be able to moor right along his woodpile."

"Very well, son, tell him to make his way back to his camp, and we'll meet him there."

The mate returned to the bow and delivered the message. La Barge glanced Adel's way and smiled. "Never can tell who you'll meet on the river."

Dawkins rode as hard as he dared to beat the steamer. Nearing camp, he saw Jim and Ezra at the shoreline, waving to passengers on the steamboat. When the boys heard Dawkins riding into camp, Jim hollered, "Bill, look at that boat!"

"It's a big one." Dawkins laughed. "Hopefully, they'll have enough room left for us."

Ezra frowned. "Bill, what about them two's horses?" He motioned to the north.

"Let's see what the captain has to say, Ezra," answered Dawkins, "and we'll go from there."

The steamer pulled along shore, towering at least forty feet over the men. The moment the boat touched the bank, a uniformed officer hollered, "Woodpile," and around twenty men leaped ashore. Then several hands operating the ship's steam hoisting winch swung an enormous stage from the derrick nearest the bank. The loading platform landed on the shore with a dull thud, and Dawkins marveled at its size, large enough to carry a four-horse wagon team with room to spare.

The mate who had spoken to Dawkins along the shore approached and nodded at the stack of logs. "That's some good work, men. Where did you clear those dead logs?"

Dawkins turned and pointed to the stand of pines behind them. "Plenty more up there. This is just a half-day's worth."

"Very good," said the mate. He ordered his men to follow, and then turned back toward Dawkins. "Captain La Barge will be along directly to speak with you." He hurried up the hill with crew in tow, and soon Dawkins heard their axes.

He returned his attention to the boat and saw two men extend a narrow plank to the shore. An older man in uniform with silver hair and a white beard left the ship and walked their way. Dawkins approached the officer, with Jim and Ezra following.

"Good evening, gentleman, I'm Captain Joseph La Barge." He bowed slightly and extended his hand.

"Name's Bill Dawkins, Captain, and these two men are the Miller twins, Jim and Ezra." Dawkins shook La Barge's hand

THE RIVER'S SONG

and motioned toward the pile of logs. "We thought you might need fuel, sir."

La Barge nodded at the Millers then spoke to Dawkins. "Of course, fuel is always a problem on the upper river. We've been running on green cottonwood for the last few days." He pointed at the logs and asked, "What did you have in mind for payment?"

"Well, Captain," said Dawkins, "We also have five elk we killed this morning hanging in the timber yonder, and we're hoping to make passage on your ship for Fort Benton."

"I see," said La Barge, rubbing his chin. "Let's look at those elk, shall we?"

Walking to the edge of the timber where the elk hung, La Barge stopped to examine the wagon and horses picketed in the shade. "Hide hunters, eh? Looks like the wagon will weigh around a ton and eight horses as well."

"Yes sir, well, actually only six mounts. We'd be leaving two behind."

La Barge stopped and looked at Dawkins. "Two behind?"

"It's a long story, but two more men will be coming along in the next day or so to fetch them," said Dawkins. He glanced at Jim and Ezra, and then returned his attention to La Barge. "They'll be riding on to hunt some more."

The men reached the edge of the woods, and Dawkins pointed to the two meat poles where the elk carcasses hung. "We killed these this morning, all young animals."

La Barge smelled one of the animals and felt the meat. "Cooling pretty well for such a hot day. You men must have skinned these right away."

"Yes sir, I mean, Captain," blurted Jim.

La Barge smiled at the young man and turned to Dawkins. "How would you men like a chance to work for your fare?"

Jim smiled at Ezra and then looked at Dawkins, who answered, "That sounds like a good opportunity, Captain. What did you have in mind, sir?"

Men from the wood detail were returning to the stage, loaded down with timber. La Barge addressed Dawkins. "I lost my two best hunters at Fort Peck. They were spooked by the Sioux and wouldn't leave the boat to hunt." He patted one of the elk and said, "That doesn't look like a problem for you men. I'll take you three on and haul your freight and livestock to Fort Benton, for these five elk, your woodpile, and your labor in keeping us in meat for the next ten days or so."

Dawkins looked at Jim and Ezra, grinning and nodding, then extended his hand to La Barge. "Thank you, Captain, you've got yourself three hunters."

"Very good, Mr. Dawkins," said La Barge, shaking his hand. "There are over two hundred passengers and crew on the *Chambers*, and we're starved for fresh meat. I daresay these five elk will be gone in a couple of days."

Dawkins glanced at all the folks watching from the three decks of the ship. He noticed a tall woman in a white dress standing next to the pilothouse. Even from a distance, she looked beautiful and intelligent, her eyes following the captain's every move. Still watching the woman, Dawkins nodded. "I understand, sir."

"Generally, you'll leave the boat a couple of hours before first light and hunt upriver, leaving any animals you kill along the river where we can fetch them with the yawl. You'll rendezvous with the ship around noon, and the afternoon and evenings are your own. I never ask my hunters to perform any other work."

"Yes sir, Captain, that sounds like a fair arrangement," said Dawkins, returning his full attention to La Barge. "I don't think the three of us will have any problem keeping the boat supplied with game."

La Barge smiled then looked upstream, where the sun still hovered over the Missouri. "Well, gentlemen, we still have an hour or two of sailing light, and it looks like our crew has collected a good number of logs." He motioned toward the wagon and picketed horses. "You should get your rig down to the bank, and we'll load it on the stage as soon as the wooding crew finishes their work."

Dawkins nodded to La Barge and walked toward the stock, with Jim and Ezra in tow. "Cut out that lawman's horses," Dawkins said, pointing his thumb to the north, "and picket them in some good, fresh grass." As an afterthought, he added, "Hang a hindquarter from one of them elk by their horses. The least we can do is feed ol' Beidler for a few days."

Near dark, Beidler and Craft stumbled along the wagon trail to the remnants of a camp made on a bare ridge overlooking the Missouri. Beidler gazed up the valley and pointed toward the river. "Look at that, for God's sake, Craft."

"Wait, I see smoke above the river…there's a steamer about to go around that bend," said the lieutenant.

"We missed them by, what," asked Beidler as he watched the boat disappear upstream, "a couple of hours?"

Craft dropped his head in exhaustion. "Now what?"

"It's too dark to go any farther, Lieutenant. Come first light, we'll drop down to the river and see if they left our horses."

"Did we lose them, then?" asked Craft. "Is that it?"

"Hell, no." Beidler grinned weakly and pointed to the west. "That boat's just as good as a prison. We know where they're headed now. We just got to get to Fort Benton before they do."

Chapter Ten

Dawkins looked at his watch and noted the time in the dim light of the lantern hanging below the hurricane deck. The *Chambers* was moored a mile above the confluence of the Missouri and Musselshell. Jim and Ezra led four horses from the steamer's stable at the rear of the boat to the bow, taking care to quietly pass the deck passenger quarters. Dawkins met the men near the open deck, in front of the fireboxes and engines, and inspected the string. They saddled three horses and led a fourth for packing game. With another couple of hours before sunrise, this was their last chance before leaving the boat to check tack, weapons, and other gear. Satisfied with the string, Dawkins led his horse off the gangplanks to the shore, Jim and Ezra in tow.

This was their third morning hunting from the ship. As Captain La Barge had predicted, the passengers and crew of the *Chambers* devoured the fresh elk Dawkins and the Millers had provided. The hunters took several deer along the river the last two mornings, but Dawkins was after bigger game this day to get ahead of the passengers' insatiable demand for wild game. Before turning in, he had told the captain they would be leaving the river valley to hunt the prairie. They were looking for buffalo now that they were able to hunt the south side of the river, where Dawkins hoped there would be less chance of running into any Indian hunting parties, or Beidler, for that matter.

Now Dawkins led his horse in the dark. The solid ground below him felt good after he had spent the last half day walking and sleeping on the rocking *Chambers*. Away from the boat, he spoke for the first time that morning. "Let's mount up, and we'll head up this little creek until we reach the top of the bench." He turned to Jim. "Should be light by the time we get up there. We'll have the sun to our backs and should be able to find some high spot to glass whatever game is about."

"Hope we can find some buffler, Bill." Jim's voice sounded tired and sleepy.

"Yeah, that'd suit me fine, too," chimed Ezra.

Dawkins laughed to himself and thought about Jim. He fit in well with the passengers and crew quartered on the boiler deck. True to his word, Captain La Barge did not require any labor of them beyond hunting, so every evening Jim joined the passengers in drinking and dancing on the bow. Dawkins remembered how he, too, had once been able to burn the candle at both ends.

Ezra, on the other hand, was still not himself. Dawkins noticed a look of pain on his face every time a pretty girl on the ship passed his way or a couple walked along the shore in the moonlight. It had only been a couple of weeks since he had lost Belle, with no funeral or any other chance to grieve. Of the three of them, Ezra had been most at ease with the friendly Red River folks. His strong, silent ways suited the Métis, who were not impressed with a lot of hot air and bravado. Dawkins suspected Ezra missed his new friends as well as Belle.

Dawkins was relieved to put a little distance between the three of them and Beidler. They had not lost the determined lawman, he was certain of that, but at least they had a week or so to gain some ground on him. Dawkins had visited Captain La Barge in the pilothouse and studied his map of the upper river. With good weather and river flow, Dawkins thought they would beat Beidler to Fort Benton. Every afternoon, when they returned to the *Chambers,* Dawkins reported to La Barge and determined their location, always wondering how near Beidler might lurk.

In the meantime, Dawkins tried to enjoy the voyage and the chance to see new country. He sort of liked living on a boat, hunting every day and having others to cook, clean, and take care of all the work a man had to do for himself on the trail. He was getting to know La Barge a bit, and since he had recognized the captain's barely perceptible French accent, Dawkins visited the pilothouse and practiced speaking La Barge's native language in conversation with the captain.

The previous evening, when Dawkins climbed the steps to the pilothouse, he passed the same lovely woman he had seen the day they hailed the *Chambers.* Evidently, she had been visiting La Barge and was returning to her quarters, which Dawkins presumed were on the hurricane deck. He tried not to stare and politely tipped his hat as she passed him on the narrow stairway. She was tall and wore her dark brown hair in a neat bun at the back of her head. Her brown eyes were fetching, and the small smile she allowed him made his legs wobble. She moved gracefully down the stairway, and the sweet aroma of wild roses lingered.

Dawkins smiled and shook his head. Too old to get set on some gal he had not even met, nor likely ever would. He hoped La Barge might mention her when the two men visited, but the old man did not, and Dawkins did not feel comfortable asking of her. He decided to look for her again on the boat and tried to keep his mind on the work at hand.

The ride out of the river valley to the uplands was about four or five miles, as near as Dawkins could figure. They had been riding over an hour when a false dawn lit the long swale ahead well enough to see the edge of the prairie. Dawkins raised his hand and motioned for Jim and Ezra to ride alongside him. "Looks like about half a mile to the top. Let's circle around to the right, and we can use that strip of snowberry yonder for cover."

When they reached the edge of the prairie, they tied their horses to waist-high brush and crept forward to look for game. From the crest of the ridge, they saw the long elbow of the Missouri behind them, where it turned to the west. The *Chambers* was already under way and would stay in sight all day. Then Dawkins turned his attention to the rolling prairie that stretched for miles to the west. First he looked close, along the ground within rifle range for any animals about. Soon he saw deer and pointed them out to Jim and Ezra, who both grinned.

Dawkins had heard from old-timers on the *Chambers* that there were still plenty of buffalo between the Judith and the Musselshell. He planned to spend most of the day looking for them.

After sunup, Dawkins rose and stretched. "Let's mount up and keep working up the valley."

"Plenty of deer and antelope, Bill, but no buffler," said Jim.

Dawkins watched the deer scurry into the brush as the hunters revealed themselves. "I'm thinkin' we can always kill our share of deer and antelope. Let's hold out until noon for something bigger."

They rode behind the northern edge of the prairie and traveled a few miles to the west. When they reached a shallow swale, Dawkins raised his arm, and they dismounted. With the sun well above the eastern horizon, he took his field glasses and rifle. "You boys just wait here, and I'll mosey up to the rim and see what's about." He handed his reins to Ezra and hurried up the ridge.

On hands and knees, Dawkins peered over the rim and viewed the rolling prairie. Several deep coulees ran in succession down to the river. To the south, a long, grassy table stretched for miles toward the Judith River. If there were any buffalo about, Dawkins thought, that is where they would be. He knelt behind a tall sagebrush and glassed the expanse of prairie.

Below the ridge Dawkins heard magpies squabbling sharply, and then they flushed toward the river. He lowered his field glasses and slowly stood to view the bottom of the shallow draw. The instant Dawkins rose, he heard a thunderous roar from the brush below. A dark blur came rushing toward him, leaving a wake in the waist-high grass like a steamer running up a river.

Grizzly!
Only got one shot.
Make it count.

Time stood still as Dawkins cocked the Sharps and tracked the silver-tipped hair protruding from the deep grass, highballing to the top of the ridge.

Before he could shoulder his rifle, the bear emerged from the brush and lunged for him, bellowing and snorting, its snapping jaws echoing like rocks tumbling down a cliff.

Dawkins shot from the hip.

Then the grizzly was on him.

The momentum of the charging bear knocked him several yards down the ridge.

Dawkins instinctively raised his rifle to block its mashing jaws. He felt its hot, damp breath and saw blood spilled from its forehead.

When the bear landed on him, its great weight knocked the wind out of him, and shooting pain wracked his chest. He heard a low groan, and the animal went limp.

Five hundred pounds of dead bear pinned Dawkins to the ground. He squirmed to free himself and tried to holler for the boys but could not breathe.

An instant later, he heard Ezra running to him. "Bill, you in one piece?" Ezra grabbed one of his legs to help pull him free. "The horses just about stampeded when they heard this bear."

With Ezra's help, Dawkins managed to roll out from underneath the dead grizzly and sat in a daze next to the huge beast. He looked into the dead bear's eyes. They still looked alert and angry.

Jim came running up the ridge. "I had to get them horses tied up," he gasped. "Bill, you're covered in blood."

"I think it's mostly his," said Dawkins. He tried to stand, and his legs nearly buckled under him. He dropped to one knee, then sat on the dead bear's back. He remembered the bear hunts of his youth in Pennsylvania. He had never been charged, let alone mauled by a bear, and he had never seen a beast to match this grizzly.

"I don't know, Bill," said Ezra. "Let's look you over some."

Dawkins's chest and left arm burned when Ezra peeled the torn shirt from him. Jim fetched a canteen from the pack string and dampened a piece of the cotton. Dawkins closed his eyes and breathed in shallow gasps as Jim cleaned him up.

"Well, I reckon you'll live, but ol' Ephraim must have clawed you some, 'cause you're torn up a might," said Jim. "You'll live until you die, ain't that what you always say, Bill?"

Both boys laughed, too fast and too hard. Ezra added, "You said you was after bigger game than deer."

That started Dawkins laughing, but then he felt the rips in his chest and upper arm. He slipped to the ground, using the dead grizzly for a backrest.

"I guess somebody back at the boat can sew you up good as new," said Jim. "Want us to get you back to the *Chambers* now?"

"Nope," said Dawkins. "Not until you got this beast skinned and quartered." He patted the bear's rump and felt about as alive as a man could.

La Barge raised his field glasses when his hunting party appeared along the ridge overlooking the south bank of the Missouri. The *Chambers* had made good time during the morning run, but a growing wind forced La Barge to make for shore in the early afternoon. He took advantage of the idleness by sending a wood party to collect fuel.

From the pilothouse, La Barge had a good view of the hunters as they wound their way down the rock- and timber-strewn hillside. As the men drew nearer, he noted their packhorse strained under a full load. So far, Dawkins and the Millers had proven to be fine hunters. La Barge was growing particularly fond of Dawkins, who seemed sensible and gentlemanly. The old captain thought he might even offer to employ the man on the return voyage to St. Louis. But something told him these men were on the run. La Barge could not put his finger on it, exactly, except they seemed to study their back trail as much as where they were headed. He guessed they would vanish as soon as the *Chambers* reached Fort Benton.

When the hunters were within hailing distance, La Barge left the pilothouse and walked to the edge of the texas. He raised his field glasses and focused on Dawkins slouched in his saddle, covered in blood. La Barge hollered to the mate supervising the wood crew, "Get some men and help those hunters back to the ship. It looks like one of them is wounded."

La Barge found one of his officers on the hurricane deck and said, "Please find Dr. Johnston. Tell her one of our hunters is hurt." Then he flew down the stairway to the bow of the boat.

By this time, the hunters had reached the shoreline. Men from the wood crew helped Dawkins off his horse. A crowd of onlookers from all decks was watching and one shouted, "Look at that bear they brought in!"

La Barge glanced at the packhorse, stomping its front hooves and snorting in fear. The head and hide of what looked to be an enormous bear covered the horse's load of meat. La Barge headed toward the plank and spoke to Ezra, who was tying his horse to a cottonwood sapling. "What happened, son?"

Jim stepped up and answered for his brother, in a high and cracking voice, "Early this morning, Bill snuck up a ridge and jumped this ol' boar off a kill, Captain."

La Barge made his way through the throng of crewman and passengers to where Dawkins sat against a tall cottonwood. "Mr. Dawkins, how are you, sir?"

"Not as bad as I look, Captain." Dawkins grinned and pointed toward the bear hide the crew had removed from the packhorse. "Most of this blood on me belongs to that bear."

Several men had lifted the hide from the packhorse and spread it on the ground. La Barge admired the beautiful pelt. "That must be seven, eight feet long, Mr. Dawkins."

"Yes, sir, and probably five hundred pounds to boot."

"Well, Mr. Dawkins, I'm very glad you got the bear before he got you." La Barge chuckled and added, "All the same, I've asked Dr. Johnston to examine you and treat your wounds."

"Yes sir, thank you, Captain." Dawkins smiled and shook his head. "That ol' griz' did manage to scratch me up some."

La Barge winced and then turned toward the shore. "Ah, here comes the doctor now." The stunning woman approached, skirts swinging around her legs in her hurry.

She placed her black leather bag on the ground next to Dawkins and knelt to examine his wounds. "So what do we have here?"

"Dr. Johnston, allow me to introduce you to my best hunter, Mr. Bill Dawkins," said La Barge. "A grizzly bear nearly got the best of him this morning."

When Adel's eyes met Dawkins's, La Barge was startled by the overwhelming attraction between the two. Looking overhead into the brilliant sky, he almost expected to see lightning crash. Maybe he was just an old fool, but there was no mistaking the instant magnetism he had witnessed. He suppressed a chuckle and ordered his crew to prepare for making way.

Dr. Johnston wanted Dawkins out of the heat and wind, so Jim and Ezra helped him to a small storage room at the end of the boiler deck. She excused herself for a moment to fetch hot water from the kitchen and a clean sheet for dressing.

Dawkins sat alone on a bench in the cool and well-lit room, with several windows along the outside wall. He was not sure what had surprised him more, his chance encounter with the grizzly or learning he was smitten with the ship's doctor. He had been treated by female army nurses during the war, but he had never even heard of a woman doctor. Captain La Barge had spoken highly of her while the boys helped him to the impromptu examining room. She had treated several of the crew members and passengers for a variety of maladies, from broken bones to cuts and bruises. That was good enough for Dawkins. Besides, what choice did he have?

He heard footsteps on the deck leading to the shop, and then Dr. Johnston entered with a steaming pot and a cotton sheet. She placed the pot on the long worktable across the room and grabbed her black bag off the table.

"Mr. Dawkins, sorry to move you around, but I thought you'd be more comfortable in here." She paused, then her face reddened. "Excuse me, I don't believe I ever introduced myself. I'm Dr. Adeline Johnston."

Dawkins nodded and smiled. "Yes, ma'am, ah, Dr. Johnston, I'm Bill Dawkins, pleased to meet you." *Adeline...what a pretty name. I wish I could call you Adel.*

"Well, Mr. Dawkins, let's get off what's left of that shirt." She took scissors from her bag and carefully cut off the remnants of the tattered, bloodstained shirt. "That's quite a bear you ran into this morning, I was looking at the hide before I came in." She finished removing the bloody garment and cut several small rags from the cotton sheet. Her touch was light and graceful, her hands soft and warm.

"Yes, ma'am, it's a big one. I'm going to give the rug to Captain La Barge as a present."

"Oh? What's the occasion?" She walked across the room and dipped one of the rags into the pot of hot water.

"Nothin' much, just a way of saying thanks for all he's done for me and the Miller twins."

"Yes, I've noticed those two young men. I thought they might be your sons. Are they at all related to you?" She gently washed the dried blood off his arm and chest. "This might sting a little, but I need to clean you up so I can examine your wounds."

Dawkins thought a little discomfort would be a small price to pay to be so close to her. "No, we're not kin, just good friends."

"You must be their leader, then." She returned to the pot and dampened another rag.

"Oh, not really," said Dawkins. "I guess I am trying to look after them, though." While she cleaned his arm, Dawkins glanced at her face. She had an inquisitive look. Her brown eyes were heavenly. She had summer-colored skin and dark hair that shimmered in the sunlit room.

"I've never treated anyone mauled by a bear, Mr. Dawkins."

"Well, Dr. Johnston, that ol' grizzly was already dead by the time he reached me, he just didn't know it." Dawkins paused. A tinkling giggle escaped the doctor's lips and his grin broadened for making her laugh. "Now, if ol' Ephraim had sunk his teeth into me…well, you'd have a lot more work here."

"Ephraim?"

"That's a grizzly, ma'am."

Dr. Johnston nodded and studied Dawkins's wounds. "Well, I don't see anything requiring stitches." She gently took his left hand. "Please extend your arm for me."

Dawkins let her fiddle with his arm while he savored her soft hand. He raised his arm over his head, and she began tapping his ribs. When she reached the middle of his ribcage, he nearly jumped off the bench in pain.

"Oh, I'm sorry, Mr. Dawkins, but it looks like you've cracked two of your ribs." She knelt to study his chest. "Fortunately, they're not broken, but I'm pretty sure they cracked."

"That must have happened when that bear landed on me."

Dr. Johnston cut the rest of the cotton sheet into long strips, about one foot wide. "We need to keep an eye on those lacerations. I'm going to swab them with some alcohol to prevent infection. Then I'll wrap your ribs with this dressing. I'll put a salve on your wounds tomorrow." She paused and added, "I'll have to see what I can find for an ointment."

"For the next couple of days, Mr. Dawkins, I don't want you riding." Dr. Johnston frowned and waggled her finger at him. "You need to rest and give your wounds a chance to heal."

"Yes, Doctor, but I'm expected to make meat, to feed you and the other passengers," Dawkins argued weakly.

"Can't those Miller boys hunt for a few days without you?"

Dawkins nodded in agreement. *I'll have them stay close to the boat, just hunt deer and maybe ducks along the river.* "Yes, Dr. Johnston, I think they can get the job done." *Meanwhile, I'll get to know you.*

Chapter Eleven

Beidler awoke before first light and glanced over at Craft, already up and building the fire. Three days had passed since the trio of outlaws had slipped through their grasp along the Missouri. True to the stranger's word, Beidler and Craft found their horses picketed near the river, in good grass to boot. The renegades had even left a hindquarter of elk. Beidler snorted out loud, thinking he had not chased men like these before. Steal your horses and then return them with some grub. And what about protecting the cavalry's flank from the Sioux on the Milk River?

Craft turned from the fire. "You say something, Marshal?"

"Naw, I was just thinking 'bout these misfits we're after," said Beidler. "I never seen the like."

Craft read his mind. "I was surprised they left our horses and this elk meat." He pointed to a piece of round that he was slicing for breakfast. "Almost seems like they want to get caught, Marshal."

"Oh, I don't think that's the case. More like arrogance, I'd say. They don't think they have anything much to worry about now that they're on that steamer."

"Well, do they, Marshal?" asked Craft. "Do they really have anything to worry about?"

"You bet they do. They got X. Beidler on their trail."

"You still haven't told me your plan," said Craft. "Last three days all we've done is ride due west, but nowhere near the river."

Beidler did not feel much like explaining his strategy for capturing the three outlaws but figured he would educate Craft to shut him up. "Look here, Lieutenant," he said as he rose and grabbed a stick from the woodpile. "The Missouri runs due west, pretty straight, for about a hundred miles." He scratched a line in the dirt near the fire pit. "Then, at a little range called the White Cliffs, it starts a big loop to the northwest." Beidler placed a small X at the northernmost point of the river and said, "This here is Coal Banks Landing. From this point, the river turns southwest and runs down to Fort Benton."

"That big loop is going to slow their progress," said Craft. "That's our chance to catch up."

"Lieutenant, just every once in a while you ain't as dumb as you look," said Beidler with a chuckle. "No sense chasin' after 'em now, not with that blasted steamer making thirty, thirty-five miles a day." Beidler threw his stick in the fire. "We'd just be wearin' out horseflesh trying to catch 'em on that straight piece of river. That's also why we're riding a ways north of the Missouri—to stay out of that Breaks country and travel where the goin's easier."

"When do you think we might be able to intercept that steamboat, Marshal?" Craft filled the hot frying pan with a couple of thick elk steaks and then looked at Beidler.

"We got two shots. First, I'm hoping we might beat 'em to this spot here," he pointed to the coarse map in the dirt, "where the river starts its jog along the White Cliffs. If we don't beat the steamer there, we'll ford the river and cut across to Fort

Benton. We're sure to beat 'em there. There's only one hitch I can think of, Lieutenant."

Craft took his eyes off his cooking detail. "What's that, Marshal?"

"They could leave the boat here." He pointed to the river a few miles downstream of Fort Benton. "At the confluence of the Marias, there's a little landing there, too." Beidler nodded. "We might aim for that spot first, we'll see."

Craft looked at the dirt map and then the frying pan. "Breakfast is served, Marshal."

Beidler fetched his tin plate and eyed the elk hungrily. "They might have returned them horses and fed us, but they're still dead men as far as I'm concerned."

Craft turned his head sharply toward Beidler, but he was cut off before he could speak.

"Besides assaulting that soldier at Rock Creek, horse stealin' is a capital offense in this territory. Shoot, I'd be within my rights and authority to hang all three of 'em summarily, just as quick as we caught 'em."

Dawkins heard Jim and Ezra rooting about in the tack room off the steamer stable where La Barge had quartered them. He chuckled at the boys' efforts to slip away without waking him. "You two better stick to hunting, you'd never make a go as house thieves." He rose from the stiff metal cot and lit a lamp. "There, now at least you can see what you're doin'."

"Sorry, Bill," said Jim. "We was just trying to make sure you got your beauty rest." The young man laughed at his own joke and went on, "Wouldn't you know it? This ol' man's tryin' to turn that grizzly mauling into a retirement."

Ezra laughed and pulled his pants on.

Dawkins shook his head and started dressing.

"What are you doin', Bill?" asked Jim. "I was just pullin' your leg. You ain't supposed to ride for a couple of days, doctor's orders."

When Dawkins bent over to pull on his boots, he winced and grunted.

"Them ribs still hurtin', ain't they?" said Ezra.

"They're a might sore, I got to admit," Dawkins answered.

"Ezra, you remember Ma tellin' us how even dark clouds had silver linings?" asked Jim with a grin.

Ezra nodded and then gave Jim a questioning look.

"Well, I figure Bill's silver lining in that tangle with ol' Ephraim is his, ah, doctor."

Ezra's look turned to a smile, and then he laughed.

"Mercy, Bill," said Jim. "She's pretty."

"No wonder he don't want to hunt," said Ezra.

"Now, fellas, you know I wished I could ride with you this mornin'," said Dawkins as he rose and finished dressing. "All the same, Dr. Johnston is a sight better lookin' than either one of you and a lot sweeter, too."

Both brothers laughed and left the tack room, followed by Dawkins. He helped them get their string of horses saddled and inspected their gear. The boat was moored on the south bank, and the crew had already extended the plank to the shore. Dawkins wiped the grin off his face and spoke to Jim and Ezra before they left the boat, "Don't stray too far from the river bottom. There's just two of ya, so keep close to the shore in case you run into any trouble."

"What's you worried about, Bill?" asked Jim as he led his horse toward the gangway.

"Being on the south bank, I wouldn't expect you to run into Beidler or any soldiers," said Dawkins, "but there always could be Indians about. Just watch yourselves. You got the scatter gun and plenty of shot. Hunt along the river and let these pilgrims eat ducks and geese for a couple of days. Maybe you'll find some whitetails."

Dawkins watched the boys walk their horses into the darkness. A minute later, he heard saddle leather creaking and the hooves of horses clicking against gravel and hardpan. He turned to return to the tack room, when a deep, jovial voice hailed him.

"Good morning, Mr. Dawkins," greeted Captain La Barge. "I'm surprised to see you about this morning. How are your injuries?"

"Mornin', Captain. I think I'll live, but my ribs are pretty tender." Dawkins looked back into the dark. The sound of the boys' pack string faded out of hearing.

"Nervous about those young men heading out without you?" asked La Barge. "I'd guess you've taught those two quite a bit about taking care of themselves."

"A man still feels peculiar sending someone else out to do his work for him," said Dawkins.

"I suppose so, Mr. Dawkins. But I wouldn't feel too bad about laying up for a day or two after a run-in like you had with that grizzly bear." La Barge approached Dawkins closer in the dim light of the lantern hanging near the stable. "Besides, I have another job for you if you're willing."

"Just name it, Captain," said Dawkins.

"Sometime tomorrow, I would say, we're going to reach a big bend in the river." La Barge paused and closed his eyes. "It's a beautiful piece of bottomland and makes for a lovely hike." He eyed Dawkins and smiled. "Dr. Johnston has been asking me for some time about taking a walk across one of these oxbows. I think we're far enough away from Sioux country now to accommodate her, but she should have a guide. Could I ask you to escort her?"

Dawkins tried to conceal his enthusiasm for the job. "North bank or south bank, Captain?"

"North."

"Hmm," muttered Dawkins.

"I understand your caution, but it's been my experience that Indian trouble, particularly with the Sioux, is very rare upstream of the Musselshell."

Dawkins closed his eyes and rubbed his forehead. *The Sioux ain't who I'm worried about.* Maybe he was being too cautious and replied, at least partly against his better judgment, "That sounds fine. I'm not sure I'd be up to ridin' by then, but a ramble across an oxbow shouldn't be any trouble." He paused and then asked hopefully, "Would Dr. Johnston be all right with me as her guide?"

"Oh, yes," said La Barge. "I spoke to her about it last night in the pilothouse. She likes the way you look after those Miller twins," La Barge said, pointing in the direction the boys had left. "I think you've earned her trust. She asked for you specifically."

Around midday, Beidler and Craft came within view of a rugged range of pine-covered hills to the north. "Those are the Little Rocky Mountains, pretty tough country that ways." He motioned to the west. "I'd say we're about halfway to the White Cliffs now." He paused and thought it through. "Maybe another four days or so of hard ridin'."

"Where would you guess that steamer is about now, Marshal?" asked Craft.

Beidler rubbed the stubble on his chin. "Probably not that far as the crow flies, maybe just a few miles to the south." He shook his head. "But we'd have a time catching up with it if we dropped into them badlands yonder."

"It just seems like we ought to be able to intercept that steamer, the way we've been traveling the last few days," said Craft. "I'm getting a little worried about straying so far from the command on the Milk River."

"Who knows where General Miles's people are?" said Beidler. "For all we know, they may have headed back to Fort Keogh by now."

"Oh, I don't know if the general is going to leave Sitting Bull behind that soon," Craft argued.

"Not much he can do if that murderin' savage don't want to leave Canada again. At any rate, when we reach Fort Benton, you can telegraph Fort Keogh, Lieutenant," said Beidler, grinning at Craft. "Shoot, I'll have to report to Marshal Piney in Helena, for that matter. With a little luck, we ought to have good news for 'em."

Beidler looked over at Craft, grudgingly admiring the young fool's grit. Still, he wondered how he had come to share the trail with such a tenderfoot. "Lieutenant, what in the hell are you doin' out here?"

Craft looked surprised and answered, "Same as you, Marshal, pursuing these fugitives."

"No, that's not what I meant," scoffed Beidler. "Why are you in this line of work—you know, soldierin' and all?"

"Why, don't you think I'm suited for this calling?"

Well, the son-of-a-buck has a sense of humor, thought Beidler. "I appreciate your gumption in tagging along, Lieutenant, but no, I wouldn't say this business is your calling."

THE RIVER'S SONG

"My father and his father attended the Point," said Craft. "When I finished grade school, there wasn't any question what lay in store for me." Craft shook his head and looked at Beidler. "My grandfather fought the Mexicans, and my father fought the South. Now, I'm fighting Indians and chasing bad men across this godforsaken country."

"It don't sound like soldiering was your first choice for a profession," said Beidler. He decided to press the shavetail. "Just what is it you'd be doin' if it were up to you?"

"Someday, I hope to be an engineer, Marshal," answered Craft.

"Runnin' a train you say, Lieutenant?"

Craft laughed and slapped his thigh. "Not a railroad conductor, Marshal, a civil engineer."

Beidler shook his head. "I ain't followin' ya."

"Engineers build bridges and buildings. They dam rivers. They might plan and construct a turnpike or design a new town."

"You know how to do all that?" asked Beidler, surprised that this fool who could barely saddle his own horse aspired to such lofty endeavors.

"Well, that's what I studied at West Point, engineering, Marshal."

"What the hell you doin' out here, then, Lieutenant?"

"That's what I keep asking myself, but I guess the army figures they know what's best for me."

"Or for them," Beidler muttered. "Lieutanant, sometimes you don't act like you got a lick of sense." Beidler looked at the young man but could not detect the slightest bit of resentment.

"People always told me I didn't have any common sense. I couldn't tie my own shoes until I was twelve." Craft laughed and shrugged his shoulders. "But I graduated first in my class at the Point with a degree in engineering."

"Good Lord," said Beidler, a new trace of respect in his tone. "Well, Lieutenant, I'll do my best to get you out of the territory in one piece. You got bigger fish to fry than this."

Dawkins waited in the tack room for Dr. Johnston. He looked at his watch and realized she was not due for another ten minutes. He felt like a schoolboy again, fourteen years old and hoping the prettiest girl in the class would sit next to him. *You fool, she probably sees you for what you are, an old man with rough edges and little sophistication.*

He saw a lot in her, though. He knew it must have been tough for a woman to earn a medical degree. He remembered how the snotty doctors had treated the women nurses in the war, bossing them around and acting mighty important. It was the nurses, though, who did the most to help broken men get through that nightmare. She must have been determined to become a doctor. The world needed more people like that.

Dawkins snapped to when he heard her footsteps, which he had come to recognize, nearing the tack room. He opened the door and greeted her. "Good afternoon, Dr. Johnston." He shook her extended hand and liked her strong grip.

"Good afternoon, Mr. Dawkins, how are you today?"

"Been pretty idle, Doctor, just foolin' with equipment and giving our horses a little extra care."

"How do your ribs feel?"

"I'm a might sore, I'd have to say."

"Let's see what we have," said Dr. Johnston. She helped Dawkins pull off his shirt, then removed his bandages and examined his wounds. "So far, these cuts and scrapes don't look too infected," she mused. "I made a salve. Of all things, would you believe it's mostly bear grease?"

"Sure," answered Dawkins. "I've heard of such, but never used it myself."

"I had to persuade one of the cooks to allow me this," Adeline said, nodding to a small porcelain bowl. "They rendered all the fat from the bear you-all brought into cooking lard. One of the chefs, a little Frenchman, swears by it for pastries and doughnuts."

As she applied the concoction to his wounds, Dawkins realized this woman was no Yankee. "Dr. Johnston, I hope this isn't too forward of me, but I hear the sound of the South in your voice…"

"That's quite all right. I'm from Georgia, Mr. Dawkins."

Dawkins winced a bit as she felt his left side. She walked behind him and placed her hand on his back.

"Mr. Dawkins, if you don't mind, tell me about this wound." She gently touched an old scar.

"That's a rebel minié ball from Chancellorsville, ma'am." Only after the words left his mouth did he realize she probably counted herself as a reb, too.

"You were lucky. That must have missed your heart by just a few inches."

"I was very lucky, Dr. Johnston. Not only did it miss my heart, but my lungs as well," said Dawkins. "While I was convalescing, I lost most of my friends."

He felt her hand pause. "In which battle?" she asked.

"Gettysburg."

"Gettysburg…" Dr. Johnston repeated quietly.

"Excuse me, Doctor?"

When she said nothing, Dawkins wondered if he had said something wrong.

After an awkward pause, she asked, "How long were you laid up, Mr. Dawkins?"

"I spent three weeks in a Pennsylvania hospital, then I got my discharge and hightailed it to Montana Territory," said Dawkins. "I'll guess and say you were a nurse for the Southern Medical Corp. A very young nurse."

"Indeed, Mr. Dawkins. I started when I was sixteen."

"I wouldn't have survived that ordeal, a lot of us wouldn't have made it without the nurses' care. Doctors did all the cuttin', but it was the nurses who did the healing." When Dawkins met her eyes, she blushed.

"We nurses did our best, but sadly, at times, I fear we lost more than we saved."

Dawkins thought he saw her eyes water before she turned away and inspected his back. "Well, I'm here, and I'm beholden to those gentle ladies."

Dr. Johnston walked from behind and cut a fresh wrap for Dawkins's ribs. "I hope you didn't find this bandage too tight, but it's important for protecting your ribs."

"I understand."

"I'll check on you tomorrow morning. Captain La Barge told me you'll be my guide across the oxbow. I'll make sure you're feeling well enough to make the walk first." She smiled at Dawkins and finished wrapping his chest.

Dawkins returned her smile and thought he would have to be on his deathbed to miss that stroll.

———

Adel left the company of Captain La Barge and returned to her quarters in the last bit of daylight. She entered her room and lit a lamp. Tossing her hat on the bed, she sat in front of a small dresser and stared at the stranger in the mirror. Nearly fifteen years ago she had planned her life's work, and she had worked that plan very well. Her drive and ambition had been rewarded with a medical degree, a staff position, and a successful fiancé.

She looked at herself and saw a woman who had never been in love. Oh, she had seen what it might mean in the time she had spent with George and a small handful of other gentlemen she had met. She had seen her friends fall for men, some wise choices, others not.

She cared for George. She admired him. She might come to love him. But there was no spark, no magic. Her heart did not flutter when she heard his name or when he walked into a room. She could imagine life with or without him. She laughed to herself when she thought of her foolish notions of romance. She had always thought she would know the moment she met the one who was meant for her.

Now Adel wondered about a rough-hewn plainsman with a gentle nature who watched over twin boys as if they were his own. A man who laughed at misfortune and enjoyed simple things like a good horse or an evening on the river.

She rose and stepped on the deck outside her room. Bill Dawkins stood on the bow with the Miller brothers, pointing toward the hills and bluffs that rose like castles and fortresses above the river, painted in reds and oranges from the setting sun. The boys laughed while he gestured and spoke, always returning his stare to the breaks or the bottomlands. She wanted to be with him. She imagined leaving the texas and scurrying down the stairways to the boiler deck. When he saw her, he would come and hold her. With her eyes closed, she felt the cool breeze, his arms around her, and the skip of her heart.

Chapter Twelve

Dawkins stood in the pilothouse watching Captain La Barge moor the *Chambers* along the northern bank of the Missouri. A few minutes earlier, they had spotted the Millers along shore, hailing the boat. Dawkins raised his field glasses and said, "Looks like the twins had a good hunt. Both the packhorses are loaded pretty heavy. Appears they found some deer."

"I told you those two could make out for a few days without you," said La Barge. "I'm glad you're on the mend and up to a ramble."

"I reckon I'm good for a few miles. Walkin's not so hard on a man's ribs as getting jostled atop a pony."

La Barge ordered the engines to a halt, and the steamer glided along the gently sloping bank. The instant the boat touched shore, one of the hands yelled "Woodpile," and the customary group of men left the boat to collect whatever driftwood and standing dead cottonwoods they could find along the river bottom. At the same time, Jim and Ezra walked their pack string over the plank to the rear of the boat.

"Captain, I think I'll go see how those fellas fared," said Dawkins, "and maybe help them with their work."

THE RIVER'S SONG

La Barge pulled a gold watch from his vest and noted the time. "They did well, finishing their hunt near the end of our morning run." The captain smiled at Dawkins and raised his hand. "Let the boys handle the horses and whatnot, Mr. Dawkins. I thought we might visit a bit longer."

Dawkins nodded and waited for La Barge to speak.

"Just up a mile or two, I'll land to put you and Dr. Johnston on shore." La Barge unrolled a map and placed it on a small table at the back of the pilothouse. "When we come around the next gentle twist in the river, you'll see where it makes a sharp turn north and then east." He tapped the spot on the map with his weathered hand. "If you head due north and perhaps a bit west, you'll have about a three- or four-mile walk across the oxbow. But it will be about twice that long for us in river miles."

"We should be able to reach the bank about the same time you do, Captain," said Dawkins as he studied the map, "maybe even a bit sooner."

"That's fine, Mr. Dawkins, no hurry, really." La Barge pointed to the timbered river bottom along the north shore. "As I said, we've had a good run this morning, so any more mileage we make before the evening sail is just icing on the cake."

Dawkins was anxious to visit with the twins and get his own gear ready to escort Adel, as he liked to call her to himself. But he waited patiently for the captain, sensing there was more the old gentleman wanted to tell him.

"I asked you to escort Adel, ah, Dr. Johnston, because you impress me as a gentleman and a reliable man, Mr. Dawkins." La Barge looked squarely into Dawkins's eyes. "I have grown quite fond of her on the voyage, and I feel personally responsible for her safety."

"We should be fine, Captain," said Dawkins. "We won't wander far from the river bottom. Shouldn't take but a couple of hours to make three or four miles."

La Barge nodded toward the bow. "There's the doctor, now. Why don't you let her know we'll be leaving here in a few minutes, and we'll be landing again in an hour or so."

Dawkins nodded and left the pilothouse. He nearly flew over the steps of the texas, through the hurricane deck, and down to the boiler level. He walked as quickly as possible through several crewmen and passengers to reach the bow.

Then he saw Adel at the front of the boat.

It was the perfect painting. The timbered banks of the Missouri framed her beneath a dazzling blue sky. The river was still smooth and silvery in the late morning light. Even from the middle of the stream, he smelled the sweet fragrance of willows and cottonwoods. Adel scanned the river, and with her back to Dawkins, he noticed her wide shoulders and slender waist. He tried to burn the image into his mind, and then she turned and waved.

"Mr. Dawkins, isn't this a fine day to leave the boat for a stroll?"

He walked near, wondering if it was just wishful thinking or if he did not sense a different look in her eyes toward him. She seemed to stand closer and more openly than before. Dawkins had always felt a little tongue-tied with the ladies, but this woman set him at ease. "It is a fine day for a stroll."

"Oh, I hope your ribs aren't too sore for this," said Adel. "Captain La Barge told me it's at least three miles or more to where the boat will meet us."

"I wish it was three hundred miles," said Dawkins. "I haven't even thought of that ol' grizzly bear since you wrapped my ribs last."

Adel blushed. "The captain said you're the best guide on the boat. He also said you were one of the best-mannered men he has ever met."

Dawkins laughed. "I don't know…if you ever got me to one of those fancy dinner tables with all the extra forks and knives, I wouldn't have any idea at all what I was doin'." He pointed from the river bottom to the prairie, which seemed roll away as far as the eye could see, like waves in the ocean. "I'm afraid I've spent most of my time on the trail. I'm not as refined as the captain thinks."

"Oh, Mr. Dawkins," Adel said as she lightly touched his arm, "don't you know that manners and being a gentleman don't have anything to do with pretentious rules of etiquette?"

Dawkins turned his head sideways. "I don't follow you, Dr. Johnston."

"What makes you all the things the captain and I think of you is the way you treat others."

She touched his arm again. He thought he would melt.

"Dr. Johnston—"

She shook her head. "I wish you would call me Adel."

"Only if you call me Bill."

Jim and Ezra greeted Dawkins as he entered the tack room to gather his gear. He removed his canvas haversack from a shelf and loaded it with field glasses, canteen, food, and the like. He paid little attention to a conversation the Millers were having at his expense.

"Ezra, you notice how Bill's been shavin' pretty near every day since we come aboard the *Chambers*?" asked Jim. "I see he even got one of the ol' women in steerage to launder his clothes."

Ezra kept sharpening a skinning knife on the workbench, and nodded with the hint of a grin.

"Shoot, I heard Bill's even been bathin' in the river," Jim said. "Next thing you know he'll be buyin' some of that lilac water—"

"All right," snorted Dawkins, "that's enough of that bull. You got something to say, just come out and say it." Dawkins fetched his Sharps from the corner and put a box of cartridges in his haversack, then he stepped nearer to Jim. "What's on your mind?"

"I'm just worried about this romance with the doctor."

"Ain't no romance, Jim. I'm just guidin' her across the oxbow as a favor to Captain LaBarge."

"Now who's foolin' who?" asked Ezra.

Dawkins laughed. "All right, is it that obvious?"

"You been runnin' around here acting like you ain't got a care in the world," said Jim. "Like there ain't the law and the army chasin' us, even."

"Not exactly," answered Dawkins. "Every time I get to settlin' in to this boat ride and all, I remember Beidler's out there somewhere, just a stalkin' this steamer."

"Ah, Bill," said Ezra. "You got a few days to enjoy things."

"Yeah," interrupted Jim, "we're just worried about what's gonna happen when we got to skedaddle at Fort Benton."

Dawkins closed his eyes and bowed his head. He had not thought that far ahead. Besides, most likely it was only a friendship he might have with Adel. But the way she had greeted him just now made him wonder. What if she had the same feelings he did?

Jim brought him back to the here and now. "Listen, Bill, if Dr. Johnston decides to run away with you, she's always welcome to join our outlaw gang." Both brothers laughed, and Jim slapped Dawkins on his good shoulder. "We got to rawhide ya some, it's too good a sport not to."

Dawkins smiled for show but wondered. *Just what are you doin', anyway, you fool.* Then he remembered the way Adel had looked at him and touched his arm and the things she had said to him. He shouldered the haversack and left for the bow of the boat.

The *Chambers* landed along a high bluff where the big bend of the Missouri began. Adel and Dawkins stood on a large stage hoisted by a steam-powered winch to the top of the bank. He extended his arm, and Adel held on with both hands as the platform swung from the derrick to the cut bank overlooking the river. After the stage settled on the flat piece of ground, Dawkins escorted her off the wooden deck. The crew swung the stage back and lowered it into the ship. Several hands pushed the boat off the shore with long poles, and the *Chambers* slowly headed upstream. The boat whistled twice, and Captain La Barge waved from the pilothouse. Then all they could see of the *Chambers* was the big stern wheel churning muddy water to froth.

Adel stepped into a clearing between tall cottonwoods and spun in a circle. "Isn't this grand? You don't know how long I've wanted to leave that boat and stretch my legs." She smiled and looked above to the crowns of the trees. "Is the walk to the other shore all timbered?"

Dawkins gazed north. "When we reach the top of this little hill we'll be out in the open for a mile or two, then we'll drop back down to the river bottom on the far bank." He removed the field glasses from his sack. "I brought these if you want to see what all these birds look like you've been listening to from the *Chambers*."

"Maybe on the other side, Bill," Adel said. "Right now I just want to clear the trees and get to that prairie I've been gazing at the whole voyage."

"Well," Dawkins smiled, "here we go, then."

When he turned to lead the way toward the hill, Adel reached for his hand and was glad for his firm grip. He stopped and gazed into her eyes. If he kissed her she would not complain, but he only paused for a moment and then laughed softly. It was enough, for now, thought Adel. The look he gave her said all she needed to know. She knew he was a shy man, but she figured he would get the nerve to take a chance by the end of the stroll.

Dawkins led Adel up the wooded hillside at a slow pace. She wore riding boots that looked well broken in, but he figured to go slow until they reached flat ground. When they made the crest of the hill, Dawkins stopped and spoke in a hushed tone, "Out here, it's a good idea to look things over a bit before you go skylinin' yourself." He peered over the edge of the rim and viewed a finger-shaped bench extending from the edge of the river to where the badlands erupted from the prairie, several miles to the northeast. He did not think it likely for anyone to be about in such remote country, but he raised his glasses and slowly scanned the prairie and the bases of the breaks.

The first hint of trouble was a cloud of dust rising from the behind a wave of low-lying hills a couple of miles away. "I don't know, Adel," he said. "There's a cloud o' dust headed this way."

He motioned for her to step up to the edge of the swale and pointed toward the brown cloud moving toward them.

"Couldn't that be the wind, Bill?"

Dawkins studied the tan smudge on the horizon through the field glasses. "Problem is that dust is moving against the wind." He looked back toward the river bottom and decided staying near the timber was not a bad plan. "We best wait right on the edge of this hill until we see what's raisin' that dust." Dawkins saw Adel's eyes widen. "Might just be buffler."

He leaned against a ponderosa pine and viewed the far end of the flat. Then he saw riders emerge from the buckbrush and junipers at the base of the distant hills. They rode in single file, and by the time they all reached the prairie, Dawkins counted eight horses headed toward them in a ground-eating lope. "Adel, you best see this." He pointed to the north.

She gasped. "Who are they?"

Dawkins guessed the riders to be within a couple of miles and raised his field glasses. He saw brown skin glistening in the sun. *Indians.* From where they hid, only a small stretch of the river could be seen, and the *Chambers* had long since rounded the bend. Dawkins wondered how to get back to the boat with a band of Indians getting closer and cutting off their way to the other side of the oxbow.

"We're gonna stay hid here and see what they're up to," said Dawkins. He smiled at Adel and looked back to the approaching riders. "There's no way they've seen us. My guess is they're following the boat. You can track one of them steamers from a long ways off by the smoke."

"Why would they be interested in the *Chambers*?"

Dawkins stopped himself before he told Adel the riders might be looking to capture or kill anyone foolish enough to get off the boat. He raised his field glasses to gauge the Indians' progress. They had reached the peninsula of prairie extending inside the river oxbow. Soon they would be nearly between where he and Adel hid and the far shore where the *Chambers* was to moor.

The Indians slowed their ponies to a walk, and Dawkins guessed they were less than a mile away. He rested his field glasses on a dead limb of the pine he was hiding behind and surveyed the band. "Adel, they're pretty close now, so it's important to be real quiet and stay right where you are there, below the ridge line."

He heard her say, "All right, but I'd sure like to take a look at them. I've never seen any Indians before."

Dawkins said out of the side of his mouth, "Maybe you can sneak a peek in a bit, but let's wait 'til they're not so close." He kept watching the riders, who had stopped and were wildly gesturing to the west. Dawkins muttered, "Parted hairs, Sioux, I reckon."

"Excuse me?"

"I think they're Sioux, judging from their hair. I believe I can see some braids swinging on a few of 'em," answered Dawkins. "They're all facing away from us. I think they're watchin' the *Chambers*."

Dawkins eased from behind the pine and dropped down the hillside to reassure Adel. He shook his head and gave her a small grin. "I guess this is a little more adventure than you bargained for."

Adel took his hand and pulled herself against his chest. "Bill, I wish I knew how you're going to get us back to the boat."

Dawkins put his arm around her shoulder and looked into her brown eyes. "Don't worry, Adel, this is a good defensive position. I can hold off a heap of 'em from here with this." He raised his rifle with his free arm. "But I don't think it will come to that." He stood on his toes and looked over the grass to the prairie. The Indians had started moving again and were riding toward the end of the oxbow where Dawkins judged the *Chambers* to be. He pulled his watch and noted the time. They were due on the other side of the oxbow in an hour. He glanced back to the Indians and saw the last of the riders dropping off the bench into the rock- and timber-strewn hillside overlooking the Missouri. Holding Adel near, he thought, *I'm not about to let anyone harm the woman I love.*

Chapter Thirteen

Marshal Beidler and Lieutenant Craft trudged along the prairie under a murderous sun, leading their horses to give the poor beasts some semblance of a rest. Beidler looked to the south, toward the verdant river valley. It would be cooler there, he thought, and shady. But the Missouri Breaks were tough traveling, so his posse of two had skirted the worst of the rock- and cliff-strewn hills to save time and overtake the *Chambers*. Earlier in the day, during the noon break, he saw a black cloud rising from the river, miles to the west. Only a steamboat could make such a column of smoke. They were getting close.

But their horses were nearly played out. For weeks, both mounts had been pushed hard with poor forage and scant rest. Fatigue also dogged Beidler and Craft. Only weeks earlier, they had pursued Sitting Bull's Sioux with General Miles, from Fort Peck all the way to the Canadian border. Then, with no rest, the brass sent them to chase three fugitives.

When they left Miles's command, Beidler expected to be gone a few days, perhaps, but not the better part of two weeks. He figured they had ridden around two hundred miles chasing these three horse thieves and ne'er-do-wells. If their mounts held on another couple of days, Beidler and Craft might reach

THE RIVER'S SONG

the river in advance of that steamship, somewhere around the White Cliffs.

Craft broke the silence of the last few hours. "Marshal, how about a short rest? I'm about as tired as these horses."

Beidler nodded toward a patch of junipers along a ridge of the coulee. "Let's sit in that shade, yonder."

When they reached the scrubby trees, Craft tied his reins to a low limb and stretched his arms. "I'm going to take my field glasses and climb that little knoll to the right. I'll take my rest up there, see if I can spot that boat."

Beidler waved him on and sat against a stubby cedar. He drank from his canteen and watched Craft scramble up the steep hill. Beidler's eyelids grew heavy as he relaxed. He was nearly asleep when he heard Craft scream. Beidler snapped awake in time to see Craft recoil backward from near the top of the rocky hummock, a rattlesnake dragging from his hand.

Beidler leaped to his feet and ran to Craft, who had shaken the snake loose but stood frozen, screaming in fear and pain. "Craft, move away from that rattlesnake before you get bit again!"

Craft stumbled down the hillside, shock and disbelief in his eyes. Beidler reached him near the base of the hill and scolded, "Sit down, calm yourself."

"I'm snakebit, Marshal," the young man cried as he held his hand against his chest and trembled. "Oh my god, it hurts." Tears ran from his eyes.

Beidler reached for his hand. "Quiet down now, Craft. Let me look at it." Beidler grabbed the lieutenant's wrist and examined his right hand, already swollen and red. Two puncture holes, an inch apart on the heel of his palm, oozed dark blood. Beidler untied his bandana and tied it above

Craft's wrist. "Let's get you down in the shade, and I'll work on this."

When they reached the clump of junipers, Beidler pushed Craft to sit against a tree. Then he pulled his pocketknife and opened the blade. "I need to cut them fang holes so I can suck the poison out."

"Are you sure?" asked Craft as he clutched his arm and turned from Beidler.

"You're damned right I'm sure," bellowed Beidler. "You can turn away if you want, but give me your hand." Beidler grabbed Craft's wrist and knelt. "This is gonna hurt some, but we gotta get that poison out." He cut an X across the first hole, and Craft shrieked and tried to pull free. "Dammit, boy, just one more cut." He sliced another X over the second hole. "There now, that's the worst of it."

Beidler sucked hard on the two wounds and spat black ooze in the sandy soil. He wiped his mouth with the back of his hand and sucked again, this time spitting less of the thick blood. With the water from his canteen, he washed his mouth out before spewing a pink froth on the ground. "It tasted like I got a lot of the venom, Lieutenant," said Beidler. "I need to bandage that hand now."

Beidler untied the silk scarf from Craft's neck and wrapped it around the lieutenant's palm. "There now, lie down some and rest that hand on your chest. We'll stay here awhile and see how you do."

Unsaddling the horses, Beidler worried about leaving the trail and letting the boat steam farther away. He looked longingly toward the river and then returned to the cedars, where Craft lay.

THE RIVER'S SONG

Beidler allowed Craft to rest an hour, then summoned the greenhorn. "We got to get goin' now, Lieutenant." When he did not respond, Beidler walked under the trees and inspected Craft's hand. It had not swollen much more, and Beidler had likely sucked out most of the poison. "That hand don't look half bad, Craft. Besides it ain't gonna get any better here."

"I feel hot, Marshal," Craft whispered. "I don't know if I can ride."

"Like hell, boy, you can ride. I'll put your arm in a sling and help you mount up." Beidler looked at the Missouri. "We got to move. Besides, could be there's somebody on that boat who might be able to fix you up."

Without waiting for a reply, Beidler saddled both the horses. He fetched Craft and helped him to his feet. Beidler made a sling from an extra scarf he packed and helped Craft mount his horse. "We don't have to move fast, Lieutenant, just steady."

Beidler saddled up and headed across the coulee. He turned to make sure Craft was following and then settled in for a long ride. He planned to travel into the night, if need be, but they had to catch that boat where the river ran north, just a day's ride ahead.

By midafternoon, they had left the roughest going and reached a long ridge running perpendicular to the river, perhaps ten miles to the south. Beidler stopped and uncased his field glasses. He scanned a long portion of the river that stretched across the prairie like a silver ribbon, shimmering in the last bit of sun.

"Well, I'll be dogged if I don't see me a steamship," Beidler hollered. He pointed toward the distant boat, just a white speck without field glasses.

Craft breathed heavily, "How much longer do we have to ride, Marshal?" His face and shirt were soaked in sweat, and he wobbled on his horse. "I'm so light-headed I can barely stay awake."

Beidler rode alongside the lieutenant. "Let me look at that hand again." The palm had darkened to a bluish hue, but it was still not too swollen. "Here, let me have your reins," said Beidler. "You just hang on to that McClellan saddle and I'll drag you along."

Beidler studied the steamer glittering in the bright sun. He calculated where to intercept the boat. He and Craft had to keep riding west and pull ahead of the boat. Sometime the next day, they would be waiting on the north bank, along a good landing. He might have to hail the boat with gunfire if necessary, but he was going to stop that steamer and catch those outlaws.

Chapter Fourteen

La Barge steered the *Chambers* around the bend of the Missouri, enjoying fine sailing conditions for the middle of the day. Down on the river bottom, a gentle breeze barely stirred the cottonwoods, and the surface was still calm. The old captain figured he might reach the other end of the oxbow before Adel and Dawkins came along. That would be all right, though. He would use the time to replenish the steamer's fuel supply, as always.

La Barge noticed a group of passengers gathered below on the texas. One of the crew waved wildly toward the top of the bluff above the right shore, and the others were nodding and staring in the same direction. La Barge peered through the window to his right and saw the object of their interest. Several mounted men were silhouetted against the horizon. He pulled his field glasses from the hook behind the wheel and viewed the ridge. He studied the riders. *Indians.* Then he returned his attention to the wheel.

An officer came running to the pilothouse and opened the door. "Captain, there's a band of Indians up there watching the boat," he said, pointing to the north shore.

"I know, I know," said La Barge.

"That's right at the end of the peninsula that Dr. Johnston and her guide are crossing, Captain."

"Take the wheel and slow her to a crawl," said La Barge. "I'm going to step out on the deck and fetch the Miller brothers." He left the pilothouse and ordered a boat hand to find the twins. He watched the riders more carefully and noticed they were staying even with the boat.

La Barge's mind raced as he analyzed the situation. No one aboard the *Chambers* had reported hearing gunfire, so Adel and Dawkins had probably not encountered the Indians. La Barge also assumed that Dawkins was aware of their presence on the bench. The captain hoped the eight riders were the only hostiles up there. So far they were only winding along the side of the hill marking the steamer, which was barely making way in the current.

Where to pick up Dawkins and Adel? What to do about this band of Indians stalking the *Chambers*? La Barge was used to acting in a bold and prompt manner. He concluded that Dawkins would try to make it to the far side of the oxbow, as planned. To give Dawkins a chance to cross the bench, La Barge would distract the Indians, then steam upstream to the rendezvous site.

The captain shouted to his first mate, "Load the cannons, and then prepare to come alongshore." He looked about and saw the Millers waiting with an officer on the texas. He motioned for the young men to come up to the pilothouse. La Barge said, "Men, we need to entice those Indians down to the shore. I'm hoping that will give Mr. Dawkins and Dr. Johnston a chance to cross that bench on top and reach the other side of the oxbow."

Jim pointed toward the cannons. "What's your plan for those, Captain?"

"I hope we don't have to use them, but my crew is loading them to cover the rescue at the end of this bend."

"Them Indians is in range, sir," said Jim. "You might run 'em off with a couple of volleys." He motioned toward the band of riders, who continued to follow the boat.

"That's an option, son, but we might also drive those Indians right into Dawkins and the doctor." La Barge turned toward the Millers. "We're going to slip along the shore in a few minutes. I want both of you to gather some food and supplies from the kitchen and stores. See the officer on the texas about it. When we reach shore, you're to leave the goods on the bank. We'll cover you with the cannons."

"You reckon they'll come off that hillside to collect their prize, Captain?" asked Ezra.

"I hope so," said La Barge. "As soon as they come down, we'll shove off and head full steam for the end of the bend." La Barge was glad the Millers had agreed to the tricky assignment but added, "Men, this is a dangerous job. Those riders up there may fire on you."

"Captain, you get this boat alongshore, and we'll unload the bait," said Jim. "I just hope we can get around the point before them warriors find Bill and Dr. Johnston."

Dawkins checked his watch. The Indians had been out of sight for at least half an hour, and he was getting restless to move toward the other side of the bend. Once more he studied the lay of the land and thought they could cross behind a shallow ridge that ran perpendicular to the bench. They would be out in the open for a few hundred yards until they reached the near end of the swale. Then they would have another mile to the timber on the far bank.

"Adel, come on up, let me show you somethin'." Dawkins took her hand and helped her to the crest of the ridge.

"Do you think those Indians are gone for good, Bill?" She looked toward the end of the bench. "They've been out of sight for a while now."

"About thirty minutes, but they'll be coming back at some point." Dawkins motioned toward the low ridge bisecting the prairie. "If we can reach that ridge yonder, we can light out of here to the other side of the oxbow, but we'll have to hurry and we need to go right now."

"What if they return while we're out in the open?" Adel gave Dawkins a frightened look and held his arm.

"If that happens we'll hide behind the ridge, but if they spot us, we'll take a stand and hope some of the men come from the steamer when they hear gunfire."

"If you think that's the best way to get back to the boat, Bill, then I trust you."

Dawkins viewed the end of the prairie one last time. "All right, Adel, let's go." He took her hand and headed at a quick walk for the end of the low rim. Every now and then, he slowed a little to view the tip of the bench. "We're doin' fine, Adel," Dawkins said while he pulled her as fast as he dared and heard her breathing deepen. "Just a little ways now, and then you can catch your breath."

Nearing the swale, Dawkins slowed and allowed Adel to pass him while he scanned the far trees and brush. "No sign of 'em, Adel. We'll slow a little and keep headin' across this bench."

Adel never stopped, but leaned against Dawkins. "I'm too scared to be tired, Bill. Those trees surely look good from here, though."

"We'll get there, Adel," said Dawkins. "Just stay low enough to hide your silhouette below this little ridge to the left." He let her lead while he continued to spy on the timber where he thought the Indians might return. Soon they came to a beaten trail, and he said, "See the horse tracks up ahead? That's the Indians' ponies. We must be about halfway across now."

Dawkins was impressed with the pace Adel kept, half-walking and half-running along the prairie. She was not a fragile woman, he thought, but brave and tough. He knew it was a crazy time for such thoughts, but he wondered how he would ever meet anyone like her again. If they reached the *Chambers*, he promised himself to tell her how he felt and the whole truth about running from the law and the soldiers. He stayed low and kept moving, waiting until they had covered more ground before studying the bench.

The end of the ridge was in sight, and Dawkins saw that it did not extend to the edge of the trees. He caught up with Adel and told her, "Slow up when you reach the last bit of this swale. We need to check the timber yonder."

When they came to the end of the gully, Dawkins told Adel to sit and catch her breath. He wriggled up to the top of the short rim and slowly raised his head. "Shoot," he muttered, seeing the Indians traveling in single file around a thousand yards away. Beyond the riders, Dawkins saw smoke rising from the river. He figured the *Chambers* was nearing the end of the oxbow. Then he looked across the remaining stretch of prairie. It gazed like a couple of hundred yards to the timber.

"Adel, we got to move, right now," said Dawkins. "They're headed our way, and we got to run for those trees." He helped her up. "Don't look, don't stop, no matter what. Just head for the timber, and I'll be right with you." Still holding hands, they bolted for the edge of the woods.

Dawkins only looked back when he heard pounding hooves and wild yelling too close to ignore. Glancing over his shoulder, he saw the Indians well within rifle range and quickly gaining ground. He and Adel were a stone's throw away from the woods, where the bench dropped off into the river bottom, but they were not going to make it. He glanced at Adel and hollered, "Keep running for the timber! Don't stop!"

Willing his pulse to slow, Dawkins turned and raised his rifle. Taking a knee to steady his aim, he saw the lead rider, a big warrior with mahogany skin and braided hair, urge his pony on. Before the Indian raised his lever-action rifle, Dawkins shot him off his mount, sending the man tumbling to the ground. The other riders slowed, and Dawkins shot again, knocking another warrior from his horse. Bullets whistled overhead as Dawkins retreated to the edge of the bench.

He knelt behind a boulder and peered over the barrel of his Sharps. Two Sioux were sprawled on the ground, their ponies running wildly across the prairie. The other Indians had dismounted and hid behind a low hummock less than fifty yards away. Every now and then, one let loose a round, but none of their shots came very close. All the same, Dawkins kept low and returned their fire, kicking up dirt in their faces, letting them know they had better stay put behind the ridge.

Dawkins was in a good position to hold off the Indians and buy time for Adel to reach the river. As long as the Sioux did not have the gumption to ride on him all at once, he could defend this ground a good long while. But how to reach the boat? The instant he slipped off the bench, the Sioux would mount up and cut him off from the river.

THE RIVER'S SONG

The *Chambers* neared the landing at the end of the bend when the Millers approached the pilothouse door. La Barge motioned for them to enter as he ordered the engines to slow and began to glide along the shore.

"We're ready to go, Captain," Jim said. "We got our horses saddled up, and we'll ride for the top of that hill just as soon as your crew runs the gangplanks to shore."

"Good, good," answered La Barge. "We'll try to cover you as well as possible with the swivel guns, but you'll be on your own if you have to crest that ridge. We won't be able to see you."

"I'm guessin' Bill will be along before long," Jim said. "But he might need another couple of guns to make the boat, 'specially with the doctor in tow."

La Barge saw the boat hands ready to make shore and told the Millers, "You better get going. Good luck to both of you." The two young men ran down the stairway at the same time La Barge felt the *Chambers* rub the shore. Within seconds, he saw them riding hard up the wooded hillside, and then he heard distant gunfire. He left the pilothouse and scanned the top of the ridge. Glassing back and forth, he stopped abruptly at the sight of Adel in her bright white dress and straw hat rushing down the hillside, a half mile away. La Barge hollered at his crew, "Get those cannons ready in case any Indians come over the ridge."

La Barge paced back and forth, nervously watching Adel and the Millers converge. When the brothers reached her, he saw her frantically pointing back up the hill. One of the brothers pulled her up on his horse and headed back for the boat while the other Miller rode for the ridge.

JIM SATTERFIELD

Looking up to the heavens, La Barge uttered, "Thank God...please save one more," and scurried down the stairway to meet Adel.

When a horse neighed behind him, Dawkins wondered if a Sioux had flanked him. Then he heard Jim holler from just beyond the edge of the bench, "Bill, you up there? Where are you?"

"Stay put, boy. I'm a little ways above you, but these bucks got me pinned down," answered Dawkins. "Just take a peek over the ridge and you'll see me, but stay low."

A moment later, Dawkins saw Jim crawl up to one of the thinly scattered pines on the crest of the hill, not fifty feet away. "How the heck are you, Bill?"

"Still kickin'. How's Adel?"

"Last I saw of her, she was riding double with Ezra toward the *Chambers*," said Jim. "Probably sippin' tea in her bath 'bout now."

Dawkins slumped with relief, then laughed. "See that knoll, yonder, about a hundred yard west?"

"Yep."

"There's half a dozen warriors laid up behind there."

"I see two dead ones out there, too."

"Yeah, them others are likely madder than hornets for that." Another errant shot whistled over Dawkins's head. He returned the fire, splattering a bullet against a boulder where gun smoke still lingered. Dawkins hollered, "Pour some lead into that hillside, and I'll scoot on down there with you."

"Yes, sir," Jim answered. A moment later he laid a steady stream of fire from his carbine into the Sioux position.

Dawkins waited until the second or third round. Then, crouched over, he ran toward the ridge. Jim continued to shoot as Dawkins cleared the bench. He made his way below a tree where Jim reloaded his rifle. "What are they up to, Jim?"

"Stayin' put if they got a lick o' sense, Bill."

Dawkins eyed Jim's horse tied to a pine sapling a few yards below. "Let's get down to the boat."

"Go ahead and mount up," said Jim. "I'm going to put a few more shots into that knoll, and then I'll join you."

Dawkins made his way down to Jim's mount and untied the reins. He climbed into the saddle while Jim fired his rifle. A second later, Jim came running down the hill, laughing and whooping. He leaped on behind Dawkins.

"They're comin', Bill. Let's get to that boat!"

They rode down the steep hill as fast as Dawkins dared, weaving between boulders and tall pines. The same moment he spotted the boat, they heard Indian war cries behind them. Dawkins and Jim rode harder. Bright flashes erupted from the *Chambers*. Cannon fire shook the boat. As Dawkins and Jim neared the steamer, passengers cheered along the decks, and Adel waved wildly from the texas.

Chapter Fifteen

The sun melted into the Missouri as the *Chambers* steamed around the last sharp bend before starting a straight run to the White Cliffs, forty miles to the west. As darkness drew near, Dawkins and the Millers finished caring for their horses and readied gear for the morning hunt.

In the confusion that followed their arrival to the boat, Dawkins had been unable to greet Adel. He saw her waving and shouting near the pilothouse, and then he and the Millers were overwhelmed by passengers and crewman. Jim and Ezra drank freely from bottles and flasks provided by the adoring crowd, but Dawkins waved off offers and retired to the tack room. Sitting on an oak barrel, he oiled his rifle and listened with amusement to the laughing and merriment.

When someone knocked on the door, Dawkins hollered, "Come on in," expecting one of the revelers to cajole him into joining the fuss on the boiler deck. But it was Adel. She entered without saying a word and closed the door behind her. Dawkins rose and met her in the dimly lit room, unsure of himself but anxious to be with her. She came near, then placed her head against his chest and held him tightly. Dawkins embraced her and felt her shallow breathing.

"It's all right, now, Adel," he whispered. "We're safe on the boat. I'm sorry. I feel like it was my fault for putting you in danger."

"Oh, Bill, it wasn't your fault." Adel looked up and smiled thinly. He thought that she had never looked so lovely. He gazed into her brown eyes and nearly forgot to breathe. When he gently kissed her, she held him tight and did not let him stop for a bit. Then she placed her head against his chest again. "I don't know what to do." She looked at him again, with tears welling in her eyes. "I promised myself I would tell you everything about me, my plans, where I'm going, if we made it."

Dawkins chuckled softly. "I made the same promise."

She looked up and exhaled deeply. "I just never thought anything like this would happen to me, I truly didn't."

"That was a close call up there, all right," said Dawkins, "but we made it."

"Oh, you fool," smiled Adel, "that's not what I meant. I mean you, meeting you, all of this."

"Adel, I fell in love with you the first time I saw you," Dawkins said softly. "I was afraid to even hope you'd ever feel the same way about me."

She whispered, "I need to talk to you, tell you everything, I must—"

Dawkins kissed the top of Adel's head and whispered, "I'll meet you tonight, after dark." He closed his eyes and savored her embrace. "We'll find a spot along the river and share our secrets."

Shortly after La Barge moored the *Chambers* along the south shore for the night, he sent a crewman to fetch Dawkins. The ship's cannons had sent the hostiles scurrying back up the ridge, but the old captain was not taking any chances. At full engine speed, he made as much river throughout the rest of the day as possible.

Now it was nearly dark, and La Barge relaxed as he waited for Dawkins. He heard footsteps coming up the stairway from the texas, and then the man whom he was starting to consider something of a mystery knocked on the pilothouse door.

La Barge smiled and motioned for Dawkins to enter. "Come in. I've been waiting all day to see you." The captain shook Dawkins's hand and offered him a silver flask. "Please join me in a celebratory tote of brandy, Mr. Dawkins."

"Sure, all right, thank you, Captain." He took what looked like a small sip of the brandy and returned the flask to La Barge, who also drank and returned the flask to his vest.

"That was a very brave thing you did today, Mr. Dawkins," said La Barge. "Thank God we were able to get Dr. Johnston and you back on the boat." He shook his head. "I don't know how I could have ever explained it to her fiancé if we had lost her." He thought he saw Dawkins wince slightly. "Are you all right, man?"

Dawkins smiled weakly. "The last few days have been somethin', that's for sure."

"I'll say," answered La Barge. "First you had that run-in with a grizzly, and now all this with the Sioux." La Barge had not spent over fifty years running passengers up the river without becoming a fair hand at reading people. He looked at Dawkins and knew there was more troubling the quiet man.

"Mr. Dawkins, I've only known you a few days, but you're one of the most interesting fellows I've ever met."

Dawkins chuckled. "I'll take that as a compliment, Captain."

THE RIVER'S SONG

"You're a dependable man, a gentleman. I would offer you employment for the return trip to St. Louis," he raised his hand when Dawkins started to shake his head, "but I know you're heading west."

"Thank you, Captain, for the thought, though," said Dawkins.

"You may think this forward of me, but I only ask so that I might help you." La Barge stared Dawkins in the eye. "What are you running from?"

Dawkins sighed and turned his head away. He gazed north, beyond the Missouri.

La Barge liked this man. But unless the captain missed his mark, Dawkins was in trouble. "I want to help you. I'm speaking to you as a friend, not just the captain of this ship."

Dawkins kept staring to the north. "We were hide hunting along the Milk. A camp of Red River folks—some folks call 'em the Métis—welcomed us into their camp."

"Of course," said La Barge, "I've traded with them many times."

"Ezra fell head o'er heels for one of the captain's daughters." Dawkins turned and looked at La Barge. "She was a beautiful young woman, and I think they would have married..."

La Barge offered Dawkins more brandy when he paused, but Dawkins shook his head and continued, "Around mid-July, we heard General Miles was headed up to the border, to fight Sitting Bull. I figured Miles would also arrest the Métis, who had been trading all summer with the Sioux."

"You were up there in the middle of that mess?" asked La Barge.

"We were there," said Dawkins. "I wanted to leave the camp and head northeast, try to avoid the army. Jim came with me, but Ezra wouldn't leave Belle. That was his gal's name."

"He was really a goner for her, eh?"

"Yep. Anyways, Jim and I took off for a week or so. When we returned, we found the camp occupied by the army. We learned Belle had been killed by a soldier. He was trying to arrest Ezra, who had refused to surrender his goods and weapons. Belle got in the way of a bullet meant for Ezra."

"Good Lord," muttered La Barge.

"That's only the half of it," confessed Dawkins. "Ezra beat the pulp out of the soldier before the other troopers stopped him. Might have killed him for all I know. Jim and I snuck into the army's camp and rescued Ezra."

"I can't fault you for any of that, Mr. Dawkins. I've had more than a few run-ins with the army myself, over the years."

"I was hopin' they'd let it go, what with all the fightin' with the Sioux," said Dawkins. "But a couple of days later, they came after us, a squad of cavalry and a US Marshal named Beidler."

"X. Beidler?" La Barge whistled low. What he knew of the man was not at all good.

"Yeah, X. Anyways, I managed to scatter most of the soldiers back to their command in an ambush, but one of 'em and Beidler dogged us all the way to the Missouri. That was their two horses that we left behind when you took us on."

"You stole their horses," La Barge's eyes widened, "and then returned them?"

"We're not horse thieves," said Dawkins. "I was just tryin' to slow them down. But I'm sure X is out there." He pointed across the river. "Trying to catch up with the *Chambers*."

La Barge rubbed his chin and studied Dawkins. A little bad luck and a big heart was all that had made the man an outlaw.

"I'm sorry for coming aboard under false pretenses, Captain."

THE RIVER'S SONG

La Barge waved Dawkins off. "I'm glad you came. It's been a pleasure having you aboard." La Barge thought, *now the tricky part.* "I guess there's something else that's happened since you joined us. Something you couldn't have expected—"

"Adel," said Dawkins. He closed his eyes and breathed deeply.

"A man doesn't captain boats for fifty years without learning about people, Mr. Dawkins. I've seen the way you look at each other."

"I didn't exactly plan for this to happen, Captain."

La Barge laughed softly. "These things have a life of their own, I know." He took a deep breath and sighed. "She's engaged to a man she barely knows, a man much older than she, a very successful merchant in Washington Territory." La Barge decided Dawkins would not make much of a poker player, watching him slump and lower his head. The man was hurting, and La Barge wanted to help him. "Well, don't they say it's a woman's prerogative to change her mind? You need to talk to her, see how she feels."

Dawkins smiled, "That's my plan, Captain."

"Before you two would ever have a future, though, you and the Millers are going to have to shake that marshal," said La Barge. "How do you plan to do that?"

"Captain, I was hoping you could unload our outfit before we reach Fort Benton."

"You think that's where Beidler will be waiting?" La Barge shook his head. "I daresay that's not his plan." La Barge pulled a map from his desk drawer. He decided to help Dawkins, maybe more than he should. But he was an instinctive sort, and something told him it was the right thing to do, for Dawkins... and Adel. "I would wager a very healthy sum that your Marshal Beidler will be waiting here to hail the *Chambers.*" La Barge tapped the map where the Missouri looped to the north, near the White Cliffs.

"I was hoping we'd beat him there," said Dawkins. "We need to sell our wagon and hides at the fort. We need a stake to reach the coast."

"From what you've told me, Beidler's been traveling north of the Breaks," said La Barge. "He should be able to reach the White Cliffs before us, especially with the time we lost on account of the Sioux. Even if he doesn't catch up with us there, he can cross the Missouri and cut across this big loop. There's no way we'll reach Fort Benton before him."

"What do you suggest, then?" asked Dawkins.

"Leave tomorrow night, before we reach the cliffs," said La Barge. "I'll buy your outfit and hides too, for a fair price. I won't have any trouble turning those things in Fort Benton."

Dawkins eyes widened and he cocked his head in disbelief. "I don't know how we could ever repay you for your trouble."

"Maybe I'm an old fool, but you deserve a second chance. You're no outlaw." La Barge chuckled, "Besides, it'll be worth it to see the look on X. Beidler's face when he learns he's been outfoxed."

Well past dark, Dawkins left the pilothouse and made his way down to the boiler deck. The *Chambers* was moored along the south shore, in a calm reach of river. Passengers and crewmen dallied on the decks and stairways, visiting and enjoying the cool night air. Gangplanks led to shore, and more people strolled along the bank or sat under spreading cottonwoods.

Dawkins leaned over the rail and watched the current, silvery in the moonlight, race past the boat. Ducks and geese

THE RIVER'S SONG

chortled and cackled against the willows lining the bank, joined in their chorus by a whistling curlew. He closed his eyes and tried to take in as much of the river as he could. They would be gone tomorrow, he and the Millers. They would leave after dark, as La Barge had suggested. Then he turned toward footsteps he had come to recognize.

Adel walked his way in the dim lantern light. She wore a wool shawl over her head. Her hair hung loose, nearly reaching the small of her back. She came close and took his hand. "Let's find a place to sit on shore." She led Dawkins to the gangway.

They walked along the bank, weaving between the trees and other groups of people seated in the short grass and scattered leaves. When they left behind the last passengers, Adel motioned to a fallen log, and they sat together, facing the Missouri.

Dawkins placed his arm around Adel's shoulder and felt her warmth. He wanted to remember this night for the rest of his life. A keepsake for the trail. The long, lonesome trail. Unlike most things, he was sure her memory would not fade.

Adel covered her shoulders with the shawl and looked at Dawkins. He had only seen her with her hair up. She almost looked like a different woman now, with dark curls framing her angular face. Her brown eyes looked like those of a doe, and her lips were full and soft. He wanted to kiss her, but there were things he needed to tell her first.

"We're leaving tomorrow, the boys and me, after dark." Dawkins could not believe what he had to say, "There's a marshal chasing us, and if we don't go soon, he's likely to catch up with the *Chambers* and arrest the three of us."

Adel slumped against him. "Why? Why do you have to go now? What did you-all do?" she asked, her voice soft and quiet against the river's song.

"The law and the army...they're after Ezra," said Dawkins. He held her with both arms and told her about living with the Métis. He told her about Belle and the soldiers and the rescue. He told her about the chase down to the Missouri. How the *Chambers* had looked like a gift from God. And he told her he would remember her until the day he died.

When Dawkins was done, Adel shook her head. "That poor girl, how sad," she said. "Ezra's so young, he'll have another chance. Someday the pain will fade to memories." Then she looked up at Dawkins, "I've learned a lot about myself on this voyage."

"Me too, Adel."

"Bill, I'm headed to Washington to practice medicine at a new hospital in Seattle." She paused.

"That's what the captain told me," said Dawkins. "You should be proud."

Adel took a deep breath. "I'm also engaged to a man I met last year in Pennsylvania. He lives in Seattle. We wrote throughout the winter, and I accepted his proposal this spring."

Dawkins remained silent, thankful the captain had prepared him for the jolt. Still, his confidence ebbed, wondering if Adel was already taken.

"I've been unsure of my decision to marry," Adel said, "even before I met you."

"Adel, I would give the world to spend more time with you, but those boys, they're countin' on me—"

"We've already spent far more time together than I did with George, my fiancé."

"Funny thing, Adel," said Dawkins with a chuckle, "our plan is to head out west too, shake this marshal."

"What will you do if you can't?" asked Adel.

"I'll get those two across the border into Canada," Dawkins said. "Even the army can't follow them across the line."

Adel asked, "What about you?"

"I'll never leave America. I'll stay here; it's not me they're after."

Adel hugged Dawkins and then looked him in the eye. "I'm not living the rest of my life with only your memory. I'm not losing you." Her eyes watered, but she went on, "You outride, you outrun, you outwit that marshal, and then you come to me in Seattle. I'll be waiting."

"But Adel, what about your plans to wed, your—"

She pressed her finger against his lips. "It's my mistake I'll have to answer for and explain, but I'm as certain about this as I've ever been about anything."

While Dawkins held Adel, he remembered all those years he had worked at the gold diggings around Helena. He had wondered what it would be like to discover that big find. He imagined it differently through the years, first with certainty and then with hopelessness.

Finally, in Adel's arms, he knew how it felt to strike it rich.

Chapter Sixteen

Dawkins arose before first light and grinned at the sight of the Millers sprawled on the tack room floor. When the boys had discovered they would not have to hunt their last morning on the *Chambers*, they abandoned restraint and reveled through the evening with some of the ship's crewmen. Dawkins decided to let the young men sleep awhile longer, at least until sunup. They were going to need their rest, that was for sure.

Dressing by the light of a candle lantern, Dawkins thought through his plans for losing Beidler and reaching Washington. He planned to travel hard and light. After last night, he was strangely excited about starting. He no longer dreaded saying good-bye to Adel. He was anxious to reach Washington, where he could start a new life with her. He was still dizzy with surprise and joy. He wanted to rush to her, but he summoned his discipline to prepare for their departure. Later in the day, when most of the work was done, he could enjoy a little more time with Adel.

Dawkins slipped out of the tack room and walked to the boiler deck. A false dawn lent a pinkish hue to the eastern horizon, but already the morning shift of crewmen readied for the first run of the day. The river was calm, and patches of fog drifted

THE RIVER'S SONG

here and there. It was colder now in the morning, and Dawkins knew fall was not far away on the Upper Missouri. He saw a light in the tack room and returned to check on the Millers.

When Dawkins stepped inside, he laughed to see Jim staggering in his drawers and rubbing his bare chest. "Dang, Bill," he said. "Shut that door, it's cold in here."

"You'll warm up fine," said Dawkins, "soon as we get to work."

"We got a lot to do, huh?" Jim rubbed his eyes and pulled on his pants. "Oh, well, I guess, I'm ready to get off this boat. Liable to sprout gills if we stay on this river much longer." He looked up quickly, as if he remembered something. "Hey, how'd you make out with the doc? She gonna join up with us?" he said with a snicker.

Before Dawkins could answer, Ezra rolled over on his side. "Yeah, Bill, tell us all about it," he said sleepily.

Jim laughed and lowered his voice, saying in an exaggerated Southern accent, "Ah hope yoah intentions ah honorable, son."

Dawkins waited until both brothers were done laughing before he answered, "No, Jim, she's not joining up with our gang…yet."

La Barge waved when he saw Adel approach the pilothouse. He motioned for her to enter and returned his attention to the river, which was becoming choppy as a morning wind rose. "Good morning, Adel," he said. "I hope you slept well."

"Thank you, Captain," she answered. "I did sleep well, like a baby."

"Splendid," said La Barge. He feigned a frown. "I haven't seen much of you the last several days…I'm desolate." He turned and smiled at Adel.

"It would be foolish to try to pull the wool over your eyes, wouldn't it?" she asked.

"Very foolish." Since he had made Adel's acquaintance, early in the voyage, he had never seen her so happy. From the start, she had been enthralled with the river and life on the *Chambers*, but there always seemed to be something in back of her mind that she could not completely bury. They might be visiting or enjoying a lovely sunset, then, like a passing cloud, her face would darken and La Barge could tell all was not right.

"I suspect Mr. Dawkins spoke with you last evening."

"He did, it was a wonderful night." Adel's smile disappeared. "Captain, do you think Bill and those boys can elude that marshal and the army?"

"He will, if I have anything to do with it."

"How is that, Captain?"

"I'm going to give Mr. Dawkins and the Millers all the help I can, Adel," said La Barge. "I'll purchase their outfit and hides so they don't have to risk stopping in Fort Benton, and I'm planning on taking them ashore after dark tonight so they can get a good start on Marshal Beidler. No one can know about this, Adel, but I've helped Mr. Dawkins plan his route out of the territory."

"Oh, Captain, I am so grateful," she said. "What sort of man is he, this Beidler?"

La Barge thought for a moment, to soften his answer and not frighten Adel. "He's a determined man, with quite a reputation…but I doubt he's a match for your, ah, Mr. Dawkins."

"If I could just know they'll reach Washington, Captain, I would be the happiest woman in the world."

"You have to have faith and pray, Adel. But I think they will." La Barge paused. "And if they do, if Bill does, what are your plans?"

THE RIVER'S SONG

"Captain, I'm not going to marry George. I pray Bill comes to me in Seattle, but, God forbid, even if he doesn't, I'm going to break off our engagement."

La Barge took his eyes off the river and studied Adel. She seemed determined and resolute in her decision. He did not see any worries, any apprehension. No frown, no grimace. She appeared calm and at peace.

Adel went on, "When I reach Seattle, I'm going to let George know that I've changed my mind. It may hurt him, but it's best for both of us."

"You may have a hard time convincing him of that last part, Adel."

"But it's true, Captain. What I've come to realize on this voyage is that I don't love him. He's a wonderful man, but I want to spend the rest of my life with someone who makes my heart skip when I'm with him."

La Barge was happy for Adel, to whom he was feeling more and more like a father. But he had to ask, "Is this blind love, Adel?"

"The first time I saw Bill, I thought he was very handsome. But it took a little longer to learn that he's well educated, patient, and kind, and he admires my work," she said. "He's a few years older than I am, but not that many." She paused. "Now that I've come to know him, I can't, don't want to even think of spending my life with anyone else. He makes me happy."

That was good enough for La Barge. This Dawkins was the right man for Adel. Now, if he could just slip through Beidler's clutches.

Dawkins and the Millers worked through the morning, readying to leave the *Chambers* at nightfall. They sorted through all their gear, carefully choosing which items to take on the trail and what to leave behind with the wagon and hides. Captain La Barge ordered his farrier to inspect their horses. The man labored in the ship's stall, replacing shoes and mending tack. Dawkins planned to take all six horses, packing three lightly with only essential equipment.

By noon he was satisfied with their preparations. La Barge had joined him in the ship's hold to inspect the wagon and hides shortly after ending the morning run. Dawkins was embarrassed by the price the captain offered; it was far too generous. But the old man insisted, saying, "In part, consider this a dowry for a woman who's come to be like a daughter to me."

Dawkins gave La Barge his grizzly rug, which the Millers had fleshed and salted. La Barge took the gift and told Dawkins, "I'm going to have this tanned back in St. Louis. It will be a wonderful trophy from my final voyage up the Missouri."

Dawkins and the Millers were packing their personal effects and bedding when they heard steps outside and then knocking on the door. Dawkins raised his eyebrows hopefully, and Jim said, "Bet I know who that is."

Ezra reached for the door and Adel entered, carrying a wicker basket. "Good afternoon, all," she said. "I thought we could have dinner together." She nodded toward the basket and smiled at Dawkins.

"Maybe we ought to check on the horses, Ezra," said Jim, as he walked toward the door.

"No, please stay," Adel said to Jim. "You're very considerate, though." She looked from Jim to Ezra, then back again. "You're Ezra, correct?"

"No ma'am, that's me," said Ezra from the corner of the room.

"I declare, Bill, how do you keep track of these two?"

"It's easy, Doctor," said Jim. "I'm the handsome one."

Adel smiled and spread the food on the workbench. Dawkins eyed the meat and cheese sandwiches hungrily. There were apples and some kind of pastry.

"The cook told me he used the last of the bear lard for these," Adel said, pointing to the rolls. Everyone laughed and served themselves.

For some time, they all enjoyed the meal and visited. Dawkins looked toward Adel in silent gratitude, and she nodded. As the pangs of worry and sadness crept upon him, he kept reminding himself this was a beginning, not an ending.

Dawkins visited La Barge in the pilothouse while the *Chambers* neared the end of the evening run. The day had been clear but windy, and they had not made as much river as La Barge had planned. "It's just as well for you that we won't reach the White Cliffs until later tomorrow," he said. "It will give you that much more of a head start on Beidler."

"I'll take every edge I can get," said Dawkins.

"How far do you really think that man is prepared to follow the three of you?"

"When we took his horses at gunpoint, he said somethin' about following us to the end of the earth," answered Dawkins.

"I'm sure he was annoyed, but surely there are limits to the jurisdiction and ambitions of a deputy marshal," said La Barge. "I hope if, ah, when you leave the territory, he won't have the temerity or the approval of his supervisors to continue the chase."

"I suppose that will depend a lot on the army, Captain." Dawkins looked west and saw the first ridges of the White Cliffs. "My plan is to give him little sign to follow. Now that we shucked that wagon, thanks to you, we won't be near as slow or easy to find."

"Stay away from towns and folks as much as you can, at least until you reach Idaho," advised La Barge.

"Once we leave the territory, I'll feel a lot better. That's for sure."

La Barge checked his watch and looked upstream. "I would say you have about an hour, maybe two." He sighed and added, "I wish there was some way to get you off the boat more secretly, but I don't see how."

"That's all right, Captain. By this time tomorrow, we'll be fifty miles away."

"Well, after we moor I'll come down to say farewell," said La Barge. "In the meantime, I'm sure you have other goodbyes to make."

Adel waited in the empty tack room for Dawkins. She clutched a small package wrapped in plain brown paper she planned to give him. She lit a candle and paced the floor, wondering how to control her emotions. She wanted to be brave and conceal her worry for Dawkins and the twins. She wanted to send him off believing their reunion in Washington was inevitable. When Dawkins entered the room, she took a deep breath and smiled.

He came to her and took her hand. "Just a little while now, Adel, before we leave." He paused. "Something I want to give you before we go." He pulled a small leather bag from his shirt pocket and handed it to her. "This was my mother's. She gave it to me when I went to war."

Adel loosened the drawstring of the pouch and removed a silver chain and cross. She admired it, and then handed it to Dawkins. "Please put it on me now, Bill," she said, turning her back to him. "I'll never take it off." After he fastened the snap, she slid the cross and chain under her blouse and against her skin. She turned and mustered all her will to say, "Thank you," without breaking down.

Dawkins took her hand and pulled her close. He kissed her, and she would not let him stop. Finally they pulled apart, both laughing.

"I have something for you too," said Adel. She reached for the small package and handed it to Dawkins. "Open this tomorrow at first light, my love."

Dawkins took the present and held Adel while daylight quickly faded and the *Chambers* moored along the south bank. Too soon, Jim knocked on the door and said they were ready to leave. Dawkins nodded and looked at Adel. "The sooner we leave, the sooner you and I will be together."

She smiled weakly, and he took her hand and kissed it. He looked at her once more as he walked out the door, then she heard his pace quicken as he walked toward the gangplank. She sat on a stiff, metal cot and cried in the candlelight.

Chapter Seventeen

Beidler rode his horse at a walk across the treeless prairie rolling down to the Missouri. An anvil-shaped bench loomed across the river, growing from pink to orange in the morning sun. He tugged on the reins of Craft's mount, urging it to drag the travois affixed to each stirrup of the saddle. The young lieutenant lay on a blanket stretched between two pines Beidler had toppled near their camp.

Craft had suffered another bad night. His hand had swollen mightily after they stopped well past sundown. He burned up with fever and complained that the pain in his arm was unbearable. It was all Beidler could do to get the lad to drink some water and try to sleep.

At first light, Beidler inspected Craft's hand while the young man faded in and out of consciousness. It was even more puffy and black, and red streaks ran nearly to his elbow. His forehead still felt like a stovetop, and he was drenched in sweat. Beidler, knowing Craft could never ride, built the travois and headed again for the river.

Now Beidler was nearing the end of the trail. With Craft's accident, the marshal had been unable to intercept the steamer the day before, as he had hoped. The lieutenant fell off his

THE RIVER'S SONG

horse more than once, forcing Beidler to camp on the prairie and give up precious ground to the outlaws they pursued.

On the second morning after Craft had been bitten by the rattlesnake, Beidler spotted a plume of black smoke a few miles downstream. He breathed a sigh of relief. They would still reach the Missouri well ahead of the boat. Only a mile from the north shore, Beidler began looking for a likely spot to hail the boat. Before he dropped down into a gentle coulee that reached the river, he studied the bank with his field glasses. Satisfied the steamer could moor along the shoreline, he rode down the swale with the second horse and Craft in tow.

Beidler always felt a giddy sense of excitement near the end of a chase. Like a hunter readying for a shot after a tricky stalk, he was anxious to hail the boat and pinch those three outlaws. He bristled at the thought of them stealing his horses at gunpoint. He doubted that when they left him and Craft on foot thirty miles north of the Missouri, they ever expected to see him again. He could not wait to see the looks on their faces when he handcuffed them.

Bad thing about the lieutenant. Figured a kid like that to get hurt, way out here in the middle of nowhere. The boy was well-intentioned but so green he could scarcely take care of himself. Beidler felt as if he had wet-nursed him forever, when it had really been only a couple of weeks. Maybe somebody on the steamer could help him or at least take him to a doctor in Fort Benton. That arm looked ugly though, and Craft might not make it that long.

Beidler reined his horse around fifty yards from the river's edge. He found some shade beneath a cottonwood, where he picketed the horses. He left Craft in the travois with his arm raised above his head to arrest the swelling. Then he fetched

Craft's rifle from its scabbard and walked downstream, looking for a high spot to hail the steamer.

Dawkins and the Millers came to a bench overlooking Fort Benton as the morning sun cleared the horizon where they had started their escape the night before. The men dismounted and stretched their legs. Dawkins figured they had covered around thirty miles, riding through the night. They and their horses were well rested, though. The last week on the *Chambers* had been easy duty, but Dawkins warned the twins that they would be riding hard now, at least until they left the territory.

"The town don't look too much different," said Jim, "than when we came up from Helena in May."

"Yeah, but we were on the west side of the river, then," Ezra said. "How are we gonna cross the Missouri?"

Dawkins left his horse behind and walked next to the Millers. "There's a ferry just a little downstream of the town." He pointed and handed the glasses to Ezra. "They should be up and about as soon as we get down there."

Dawkins walked back to his mount and fetched the package Adel had given to him. "Boys, how about we take a short rest here before we drop down into the valley?"

"Sounds good to me," said Jim. "We ain't stopped all night."

"We'll cross that river this morning and take the Helena Hill Road out of town," Dawkins said as he pointed toward the base of a steep bluff west of town. "Once we get up there, we'll take the Mullan Road all the way to Washington."

"Hoorah for that," cheered Jim.

THE RIVER'S SONG

Dawkins shook his head and grinned. Although they had been up all night, the Millers were still raring to go. The excitement of leaving was wearing off for him, though, and he wanted a short rest. He had been itching to open Adel's package since sunup but had resisted the temptation until now. He walked away from the twins and found a waist-high boulder to sit against and examined the gift.

Adel had wrapped it neatly in thick paper and twine. He admired her attention to detail and carefully untied the bowknot. Unfolding the paper, he found a small wooden box that contained a gold pocket watch wrapped in velvet. He opened it and found the inscription, "To the one I love," on the inside of the lid.

There was also a letter, three pages long, written in her flowing handwriting. Dawkins glanced over toward the Millers, seated on the edge of the bench, and then he returned to the letter. As he read, he realized Adel had written it over several days, more like a diary. She wrote about the first time she thought he might be her special one, when she saw him walking to the pilothouse after dark. She told him how brave he had been to send her on to the *Chambers* while he stayed behind to hold off the Sioux. She described their evening along the Missouri in meticulous detail.

"This watch was my father's, given to him as a wedding gift from my mother," Adel wrote. "I nearly gave it to the wrong man. Now I know it was meant for you. I'm meant for you, too."

Dawkins clutched the letter, smelled the perfumed pages, rubbed his wet eyes, and then read the last of Adel's writing. "I'll pray every day for you and the boys. At sunset, when the Missouri laps against the *Chambers*, I'll remember our last night together. And when I reach Seattle, I'll be looking east, waiting for you to return to my arms."

Captain La Barge piloted the *Chambers* past a tall, flat-topped hill known as Last Chance Bench. Across the river, on the north bank, the White Cliffs guarded the Missouri, awash in fiery reds and oranges of the rising sun. From the edge of the escarpment, the prairie sloped gently down to the riverbank, where scattered cottonwoods stood. At the base of one small copse of trees, La Barge saw two horses. An instant later, he saw a small plume of white smoke farther downstream. Through his field glasses, he saw a man waving with both arms, perhaps a quarter of a mile away. La Barge sounded his whistle twice and considered where to moor.

The old captain knew who was hailing the *Chambers*. He even thought for a moment that he might steam ahead, as if he had never seen the stranger along the shore. But other passengers and crew would notice the man and wonder. Besides, he thought thankfully, Dawkins and the Millers were long gone, probably near Fort Benton by now. La Barge informed an officer they would land and talk to whoever that man was. He ordered the engines slowed to a crawl and steered toward shore.

When La Barge felt the boat rub against the bank, he left the pilothouse in care of one of his officers and made his way down to the bow. A man with a silver badge affixed to his vest approached the gangway hollering, "I am United States Deputy Marshal X. Beidler. I need to speak to the captain immediately."

THE RIVER'S SONG

After the boat came to rest, the crew extended the gangplanks, and La Barge walked to shore. "I'm Captain La Barge, how can I be of assistance?" he said, nearing the marshal.

"I have a wounded man with me, snakebit two days ago. He needs whatever medical attention you can provide." Beidler pointed toward the two horses La Barge had spotted earlier. "I'm also looking for three men—three outlaws—that I believe to be on board your boat, Captain."

La Barge bristled at the bold little man. He brushed past Beidler, paying no attention to him, and headed toward the horses. He heard footsteps in the gravel behind him and hurried to the travois he now saw rigged to one of the mounts. La Barge knelt and looked at the wounded soldier.

Beidler came up behind him. "He's in a bad way. I tried to suck out the poison, but his hand and arm still look like hell." The marshal cleared his throat. "About those three outlaws—"

"Men," La Barge interrupted, "get a hold of the blanket and let's take this man to the tack room for now." Before Beidler could speak again, La Barge added, "One of you find Dr. Johnston."

"Now, what's this about three outlaws, Marshal?" La Barge asked.

"We'd been tracking three men all the way down from the Milk when we lost them near Timber Creek 'bout a week ago," said Beidler.

La Barge rubbed his beard. "Well, yes, that's near the location where we took on three hunters, but I don't know anything about them being outlaws."

"They're wanted by the law, all right," Beidler hissed. "And by the army, for horse thievery and assaulting a soldier. I want to see them right now, Captain."

"I'm afraid that's impossible," said La Barge as he walked back to the *Chambers*. "They left my ship yesterday."

Adel reached the tack room at the same time the crew's roustabouts carried the wounded soldier on deck. She asked one of the mates to fetch bedding and blankets from the texas. Then she instructed the men to place the soldier on the stiff, steel cot. The same cot where Dawkins had slept.

Adel opened all the window curtains of the outside wall as well as the door to provide ample light. She knelt beside the man she recognized to be a lieutenant from his uniform and removed his arm from the sling about his neck. The young officer was unconscious and drenched in sweat. She was shocked to see how swollen the hand was, nearly twice its normal size. The puncture wounds and the incisions across them oozed a dark, thick discharge. Most worrisome to Adel's eye, though, were the angry red streaks flaring from the hand toward the elbow.

Her light was blocked when Captain La Barge stepped in the room and motioned for the others inside to leave. He stopped the last mate and said, "Son, until I tell you otherwise, I don't want anyone to come into this room."

The young man nodded and stepped outside, closing the door behind him.

La Barge waited a moment then asked, "Adel, how is he?"

"Well, Captain, it's not good." She shook her head.

"You know, of course, that this fellow is one of the men after Bill and the boys. The other, the little runt of a marshal, is waiting on the deck."

"I understand," said Adel, almost absentmindedly, as she examined the lieutenant.

"I can't compel you to help him, but—"

"Of course, I'll treat this man, Captain. I took an oath."

"Adel, be careful not to let Beidler find about your, ah, feelings for Bill. The less he knows, the better."

Adel nodded and rose from the lieutenant's bedside. "I'm going to need some help here, Captain." She paused. "I want some of your hands to undress this man down to his drawers and make a bed for him on the cot. I'll require some boiling water, too." Then she shook her head, "I should talk to Marshal Beidler, find out when all this happened, and how he treated this snakebite."

"He already told me this man, Craft is his name, was bitten two days ago," said La Barge. "He thought he sucked out most of the venom."

"I can see that, Captain. The problem doesn't appear to be from the venom, but blood poisoning." Adel pointed to the red streaks along Craft's arm.

"Do you think you can save him?"

"Oh, I think so, although he's in shock." Adel returned her attention to Craft. "He may lose that hand, though."

La Barge winced and then opened the door. Adel heard him order some men to enter and help her. Then she heard a loud, gruff voice from the deck. "Captain, I need to speak with you and the doctor, right now."

Adel was surprised at the lack of respect for La Barge's position, and then she realized the crude man must be Beidler.

La Barge nodded at Adel and turned toward the door. "Come in, Marshal."

Adel knelt by Craft so she would not have to greet the marshal. When he entered the room, she was surprised by his small stature. He removed his wide-brimmed hat, revealing his shiny, bald head. He had a big, droopy mustache and several days of whiskers. A silver badge glinted on his vest.

"We can't stay long, if it's true those three men have left your ship," Beidler said to La Barge.

Before the captain could respond, Adel stood and walked toward Beidler, towering over the diminutive lawman. "This man can't ride. He's under my care now, and he's going to stay right here until I say differently." Out of the corner of her eye, she saw La Barge rub his face to hide a smile. She added, "I suspect a large part of the problem is that this young man was pushed too hard since his accident—"

La Barge interrupted her, saying, "Marshal, we're going to have to get under way. I have a schedule to keep. Lieutenant Craft is going to stay with us until Dr. Johnston says otherwise. You have the choice of staying on the *Chambers* or leaving, but you'll have to decide now."

"Now wait a minute, Captain," said Beidler, his face turning dark red. "I'm a United States Marshal. I don't take my orders from a boat captain or any woman…"

Adel's mouth dropped, and she cocked her head. Then she saw La Barge chuckle and understood why he had managed to captain boats for fifty years.

"Certainly, Marshal, you're aware of maritime law. As captain, I command this ship," he said with a smile. "You have every right to do as you see fit. But for now, the lieutenant will have to remain with us." La Barge shook his head. "By the way, I beg your pardon, Marshal, I forgot to introduce you to Dr. Johnston."

Adel nodded dutifully, then returned her attention to Craft. What she had seen of the marshal was disquieting, to say the least. But as long as the little banty rooster of a lawman was

THE RIVER'S SONG

on the *Chambers*, he could not pursue Bill, so she hoped Beidler stayed.

———⊳●⊲———

Beidler paced pack and forth at the bow of the *Chambers*. With reluctance, he decided to remain onboard rather than take his chances in the field. The captain had told him they should make Fort Benton in two days, three at the most. Even if he had taken off for the three outlaws, he would have ridden a horse nearly played out. On the other hand, the men he chased would have fresh mounts after a week of lollygagging in the ship's stable with good forage. The outlaws would be well rested too.

Beidler had never intended to take Craft from the boat. Shoot, he was a liability and had been since the beginning. But it rankled him that a steamer captain and some woman doctor had tried to tell him what to do.

He figured the men he was after would be heading west, probably through Fort Benton. So they had a couple of days' head start. He guessed they had ditched their wagon, so they would be even harder to find.

But Beidler had a plan. He would put his detective skills to use over the next couple of days to determine who these men he had trailed over the last two hundred miles actually were. Names, physical descriptions, occupations, and such. Most importantly, he needed to ferret out their likely destination. When the *Chambers* landed at Fort Benton, he would telegraph Marshal Piney in Helena with what he found. Then he would get back on their trail.

Craft would be lucky to survive. If he did, the army would probably send him back to the Milk River landing on the steamboat's return to St. Louis. Either way, he was out of Beidler's way and good riddance.

Already, Beidler was forming some opinions of the captain, and that lady doctor, too. Neither one of them seemed too happy to see him or very helpful. Captain La Barge was a pompous son-of-a-buck, a saucy Frenchman, of course. And the doctor, although she was quite a looker, seemed to be in on something with La Barge. No doubt they were both already underestimating him.

Beidler resigned himself to reach Fort Benton by steam. He could rest and pamper his horse. He had a terrible dry, what with the whiskey running out days ago. Sure to be a bottle on the *Chambers*. And with the information he gleaned from crew and passengers, he would find those outlaws if it was the last chase he ever made.

Chapter Eighteen

Adel spent the afternoon caring for Lieutenant Craft. After the mates stripped him to his skivvies, they laid him in the bed she had made in the tack room. Someone fetched a wooden chair so she could sit while examining her patient, and then the men left and returned to their duties.

One of the cooks, an old Frenchman, brought her hot water and coffee and checked on her regularly throughout the day. While Craft remained unconscious, she bathed him, cleaning away days of dust and sweat. She wrapped him in dampened towels to lower his fever and slowly replenished his body fluids by giving him water a teaspoonful at a time.

To treat his bitten hand, she wrapped it in heated compresses, which she changed hourly. She propped the bandaged hand high above his head to reduce the swelling. She watched for the infection to spread throughout the arm, but as the hours passed, Craft's arm did not seem to worsen.

When the room darkened in early evening, Adel lit two lanterns and examined Craft. She freshened the small towels resting on his forehead and felt his temperature. Still warm, she thought, but he was holding his own. She was almost certain she would have to amputate his right hand to save the arm and, possibly, his life.

Adel shuddered, remembering her service in the medical corps. At sixteen, she had seen wagonloads of severed limbs. With no anesthesia, thanks to the federal blockade, men shouted, screamed, and whimpered during their surgeries. She could still hear them crying for their mothers. She shook her head and returned her attention to Craft. At least she could give him the care he needed without the rush of an assembly line. Adel was standing in the corner of the room, by the workbench where she kept the hot water, when Craft awoke.

"Where am I?" he said in a weak, scratchy voice. He raised his head and looked toward Adel. "Who are you? Where am I?"

Adel walked to the cot and replaced the towel on his forehead. "I'm Dr. Johnston. You're on the *Chambers*, a steamship headed to Fort Benton."

Craft cleared his voice. "How long have I been here?" He looked around the room and seemed to notice for the first time that his arm was bandaged and bound above his head.

"Marshal Beidler brought you to us early this morning," Adel said. "You were bitten by a rattlesnake two days ago, don't you remember?"

"Now I do, yes, ma'am," said Craft. He rubbed his eyes and shook his head.

"Are you thirsty?"

"I could drink a river."

"I can't let you have too much water at once, but drink this." Adel sat next to Craft and tilted his head. She placed a cup, half full of water, to his mouth, and he drank it in an instant.

"How do you feel, Lieutenant?" Adel stood and unwrapped his bandage.

"I don't feel as hot, but my hand is throbbing. It hurts."

"That's why I elevated your arm, to reduce the swelling and the pain." She examined his hand. The swelling had subsided a little, but it was still black and purple, with red flames threatening the arm. She sat again and rubbed her forehead.

"How am I?" he asked. "What are you going to do?"

"Lieutenant, you have blood poisoning in your hand...I'm afraid it will spread to your arm if I don't...operate soon."

"Operation? What would you do?"

Adel held Craft's left hand. "To save your arm, and possibly your life...I need to amputate your hand." She cut him off from speaking and said, "I have an anesthetic; it won't be as painful as you'd think."

Craft's eyes welled, and he looked up at the ceiling and then at Adel. "Please don't take my hand. I'll never be a soldier, I'll have to resign, please don't..."

Adel grimaced. She was grateful there was not a warehouse of other patients awaiting care. "I'll stay with you through the night. I'll wait until the morning to operate, unless the infection spreads. Now try to sleep."

Craft nodded weakly and rested his head on the pillow.

Adel rose and rubbed the stiffness from her neck. Through her blouse, she felt the silver cross on her chest. Then she left the tack room to go to dinner and report to Captain La Barge.

Beidler made his way to the bar after having supper with the rest of the passengers in steerage. He bought a bottle of whiskey and took a seat next to the railing overlooking the river. The boat was moored along the north shore, only a few miles downstream from Coalbanks Landing. With decent sailing conditions, they would reach Fort Benton by tomorrow night, or the following morning at the latest.

He poured three fingers of the rotgut liquor into his glass and took a stiff drink. The whiskey burned going down, as it always did, and his face tightened for a moment. After a dry week, the alcohol went right to his head, and he felt warm and relaxed. He enjoyed the cool air and thought about what he had learned so far.

A couple of no-account roustabouts told him earlier the *Chambers* had moored on the south bank the previous evening. They saw three men leave the boat on horseback with a pack string. That firmed up Beidler's hunch the men were headed to Fort Benton. It was the best place to cross the Missouri on the ferry downstream of town. They were there already, and maybe points beyond, by now. Beidler asked around and learned the three men had been hunting the last week for the boat, in the captain's employ.

Beidler soon got the impression a lot of the crewman and passengers liked these men. Some folks were tight-lipped when he asked them about names and descriptions and the like. But he had the evening and another full day to dig up more information.

He filled his glass again and took another drink. The whiskey was not half-bad—pretty good, really. He was feeling more confident now about his prospects and felt like talking. Liquor always loosened his tongue.

When he saw an off-duty crewman at the bar digging through his pockets for the price of a drink, Beidler held up the bottle and hollered, "Over here, pardner, I'm buyin', git ya a glass."

A young fellow, maybe twenty, nodded and headed toward Beidler.

THE RIVER'S SONG

"Sit yourself down." Beidler motioned toward an empty chair next to the railing. "Have a snort, son." He poured the crewman's glass full of the amber-colored drink. "Name's Beidler, but my friends call me 'X.'"

The man sat and sipped the whiskey. "My name's Jones, the crew calls me 'Jonesy.'" He nodded and grinned. "Thanks for the drink."

Beidler clinked his own glass against the young man's. "Let's drink to friendship." He downed his whiskey and watched Jones follow suit. He filled the man's glass again. "Your toast, Jonesy."

Jones laughed. "Here's to getting to Fort Benton and the hell off this damned boat." He downed his drink and glanced at the bottle.

Beidler filled Jones's glass and sipped his own. "Don't sound like you've had a good voyage. Ain't you steamin' back down to St. Louis?"

"Shoot, no, I ain't cut out for this business," said Jones. "You got to work your tail off around here—woodhawking, loadin' and unloadin'—and all the while them steam engines rumblin' so loud a body can never sleep."

Beidler nodded sympathetically. *This pup can't hold his liquor.* "What do you know about them three hunters your captain brought on 'bout a week ago?" He topped off Jones's glass.

"Thank you kindly, X," said Jones. "That's Dawkins and his boys you're talking 'bout."

"Yeah, Dawkins," said Beidler, snapping his fingers. "What was his first name? It don't quite come to mind."

"Bill, Bill Dawkins."

"Yeah, that's it. I met him once, but I'm having a hard time putting a finger on what he looked like."

"Tall fella." Jones wobbled in his chair and slurred his words. "Maybe forty or so. Pretty lean, brown hair goin' to gray."

"Yeah, now I remember," said Beidler. "Them other two, his boys, can't recollect—"

"Naw, they ain't really his kin," said Jones. "Just a couple of strays he musta picked up along the ways. Can't miss them two, though," he laughed. "They're twins. The Miller brothers, Jim and Ezra. We got drunk one night together."

"So they took off the other evenin', I heard," said Beidler.

"Yeah, surprised the heck out of me when they didn't come back today." Jones shook his head and laughed.

"How's that?" Beidler dribbled a little more whiskey in Jones's glass.

"I figured they was just huntin', but I can't believe they didn't come back."

"How come?"

Jones glanced left and right and then leaned toward Beidler. "Everybody on the ship knows Dawkins and that lady doctor are sweet on each other." Jones winked and chuckled.

"How 'bout that," Beidler snorted. He filled Jones's glass and stood. "Well, pardner, it's gettin' kind of late for this ol' man, think I'll turn in." Beidler took his bottle and headed for his bunk in steerage.

After Adel ate supper and visited with Captain La Barge, she returned to the tack room. She brought a bowl of soup, hoping Craft might be regaining his appetite. Craft was her first snake-bite victim, but she remembered her training at the Women's

THE RIVER'S SONG

Medical College of Pennsylvania. Her professors had taught her to provide lots of encouragement and plenty of good food. That made sense to her, although they also mentioned giving the patient copious quantities of whiskey, which she decided to forego.

When she entered the room, she was glad to find Craft awake and alert. "Is that for me, ma'am?" he asked. "I could eat a horse."

Adel set the soup down on the workbench. "I did bring this for you, Lieutenant. I was hoping you would feel like eating. First, let me take a look at your hand, and then I'll feed you."

Adel untied Craft's sling and lowered his arm. She gingerly unwrapped the compress and held her breath. "Oh, Lieutenant, your arm looks better." His hand was discolored, but she thought the swelling had diminished and the red flames running up his forearm were nearly gone. "This is very good." She removed the wet towel from his forehead. "Your fever is down as well."

Craft exhaled deeply. "Does this mean you won't—"

"Let's just wait and see, Lieutenant." Adel fetched the soup and sat next to Craft. "For now, let's see how you do with this, and then I'll change your compresses."

"Thank you, ma'am, I don't know what to say. You're like an angel to me."

Adel laughed. "Try this, now, Lieutenant." The young man was ravenous, but she slowly fed him the soup. He was such a sweet boy, she thought. How could he really be after Bill and the twins? He did not look like much of a soldier. He was tall but scrawny, with a mop of sandy blond hair. His blue eyes were piercing, though, and Adel guessed he was bright.

"Lieutenant, how long have you been in the army?" Adel asked as she placed the empty bowl on the workbench.

"I just graduated from the Point, ma'am, ah, Doctor, last May."

"My goodness, and now here you are," said Adel. "I know how you feel, though. I just graduated from medical college in Philadelphia." She almost mentioned her new position in Seattle but remembered Captain La Barge's warning about keeping her plans a secret. She removed the compress from Craft's arm and placed it in the hot water pan on the workbench.

"We're both a long ways from home, Doctor."

"When you went to West Point, is this what you imagined you would be doing?"

"I was hoping to be an engineer, but they needed officers for a troop of recruits in Missouri," said Craft. "We all steamed upriver to join General Miles's command in June. I've been chasing the Sioux all summer."

Adel returned to Craft and wrapped his arm in the fresh compress. "How did you end up here, then?"

"My troop was pretty green, we brought up the rear on the way to the Canadian border. When they needed a squad of cavalry to go with Marshal Beidler after some civilians, they sent me."

Adel let Craft drink another cup of water. She felt a little guilty to pry, but she had to ask, "Who were you sent after, Lieutenant?"

"We don't know their names, Doctor, but one of the men was in our custody, at a camp along the Milk River. The other two men helped him escape in the middle of the night."

Adel wiped Craft's mouth and placed a cool towel on his forehead. "Why was the man being held prisoner at your camp in the first place?"

"He attacked a soldier, Doctor, nearly killed him."

THE RIVER'S SONG

Adel slumped in the chair. She hoped Craft did not notice. Bill had told her this might be the case, but he was not sure. "Do you know why this man fought the guard?"

"I wasn't there, Doctor, but I heard it had something to do with our troopers trying to confiscate his property."

Craft looked tired now. Adel knew he had been through an ordeal since being bitten. Beidler had nearly killed him catching up with the *Chambers*. She decided to let him rest.

"Lieutenant, I'm going to stay here tonight. I think we may have that infection on the run."

"Yes, ma'am," Craft said in a weak voice with his eyes closed. "I still think you're my angel."

Near dawn, Adel stirred from her chair next to Craft. After changing his compresses and towels on the hour since sundown, she had fallen asleep sometime after midnight. When the book on her lap fell to the floor, she awoke and rubbed the sleep from her eyes. She lit the lamp hanging near the cot and removed the damp towel from Craft's forehead. She felt his temperature and realized the fever was gone. When she rubbed his cheeks to be sure, Craft awoke.

"Good morning, Doctor." The color had returned to his face, supplanting an ashen gray. He looked bewildered for a moment, his eyes shifting about and then settling on his arm. "Doctor, my hand, it doesn't hurt anymore." He breathed quickly. "The throbbing's stopped."

Adel held her breath and removed the compress. The discoloration was gone as well as the swelling. His hand looked like an empty sack, with loose folds of skin remaining from being stretched like the head of a drum for the last three days.

She carefully removed his arm from the sling and showed him. "Lieutenant, you're not going to lose that hand. I never would have believed you would recover so soon. It must have been the hourly compresses, along with all the water and rest." She shook her head and smiled.

Craft's eyes welled with tears. "Oh, my God, thank you," he cried. "I can't believe it…I prayed and prayed for this." He closed his eyes and gingerly rubbed his hand.

"It's still going to be sore for some time," Adel said, "but I'm going to bandage it now, and then I want you to rest."

Adel applied a salve to Craft's hand and wrapped it lightly in a strip of cotton sheet. "I don't want you to leave this bed until I tell you otherwise, probably at least until we reach Fort Benton. We don't want you to regress, so you just catch up on your rest."

Craft nodded with his eyes closed and lay on his back, his arm resting on his chest.

"I'll be back in a few hours," said Adel. "I'll bring you some breakfast."

She left the tack room and headed toward the hurricane deck. Rounding the corner, she nearly ran into La Barge. "Excuse me, Captain, I should not be so absentminded."

"Good morning, Adel," he said. "How's your patient?"

"I declare, Captain, but would you believe he's all but healed already? Yesterday, I thought he was going to lose that hand, but not now."

La Barge smiled. "That young man is very lucky, he has a fine doctor."

Adel blushed. "Thank you." She thought about her appearance at the moment, having sat up most of the night in a stiff, wooden chair. She brushed a curl from her eye. "I must look a fright, Captain."

"Nonsense, Adel, you look lovely as always." He winked and added, "I'm sure Bill would agree."

Adel's smile faded. She looked toward the river shrouded in early morning fog. "I miss him already."

La Barge stepped next to Adel and stared across the river with her. "It's all right, dear, soon you'll be together in Seattle. Just have faith and be patient. You know you can count on Bill."

Beidler stepped away from the corner of the walkway, where the aisle ran to stairs leading to the second deck. He had risen early, unable to sleep any longer, and thought he would stretch his legs on the shore. When he heard voices near the tack room, quietly he stepped onto the wooden deck and eavesdropped on the lady doctor's conversation with La Barge.

To be sure they did not know of his presence, Beidler made an about-face and returned to his bunk on the boiler deck. He chuckled at his good fortune. Between Jones and La Barge, he had learned just about everything he needed to know.

Chapter Nineteen

Dawkins stirred from his bedroll and pulled on his boots. He rose and walked to where the horses were picketed. In the grove of poplars and cottonwoods, where he and the Millers had spent the night, their view of the eastern horizon was blocked. But thin clouds overhead, colored in pink and red, betrayed the new day, and Dawkins was restless. He would let Jim and Ezra sleep a little longer, though, while he boiled water for coffee and fried loin steaks from a whitetail doe Jim had shot the day before.

So far, they were making good time, thought Dawkins. They had crossed the Missouri yesterday morning without a hitch, riding the ferry downstream of Fort Benton. They passed through town, like any of a dozen other pilgrims. Without stopping for any reason, they followed a steep road out of town to the west that led them to the Mullan Road. Then they headed south.

Jim and Ezra talked big about riding all the way through the territory without sleep, but by late in the afternoon they were sagging in their saddles. Seeing the Great Falls of the Missouri piqued their interest, and they stopped to look down into the river canyon to admire the view. The slanting sunlight of late afternoon cast rainbows where the river crashed from

THE RIVER'S SONG

the falls above, and a good breeze cooled them after hours on the hot trail. Dawkins pushed them a little ways farther until they reached the north bank of the Sun River. There they left the road and walked in the shallows of the Sun for at least a quarter mile until they came to a likely camping spot in the bottomland.

Dawkins called it a masked camp. By riding in the river, they left no trail. Their fire was screened from view by tall, leafy cottonwoods and fed with only dry wood that raised little smoke. Dawkins had told the boys they would have to be stealthy now, at least until they left the territory. Beidler should be reaching Fort Benton any day and would soon be on their trail. They had a good head start, but they could not outrun the telegraph messages he might send to points ahead of them.

In the growing light, Dawkins checked the stock, picketed on lush grass. With three pack animals, none of the horses carried much more than a hundred and fifty pounds. Not a bad load for well-rested animals traveling on a graded wagon trail.

He drank from the river and washed his face and the sleep from his eyes. He scooped a bucket of the cold water and returned to camp.

Dawkins was pleased to see Ezra up and building a fresh fire from last night's coals. "Mornin', Bill," he said. "How far you reckon we made yesterday?"

"Around fifty miles," answered Dawkins. "Today we'll reach the Dearborn and then some. Tomorrow, we ought to be climbing Mullan Pass." He filled the coffeepot from the bucket and then set it on a flat rock near the edge of the fire. Dawkins stretched and took a deep breath. "It'll be good to be in the high country again."

"Any country where we ain't bein' chased is gonna look good to me, Bill."

"I know, Ezra. Seems like we been on the run forever, but it's really only been a few weeks." The pot was steaming, and Dawkins knelt to make coffee. "Runnin' is hard on a man."

"Don't look to bother brother Jim," said Ezra, nodding at a still lump beneath a blanket.

Dawkins was not sure if he should say it, but he did. "Ol' Jim ain't been through all the troubles you have, Ezra."

"You mean Belle, don't ya."

Dawkins nodded and handed Ezra a cup of coffee. "Don't burn your tongue."

"Sometimes I think on it and it makes me angry," said Ezra. "Now, though, I mostly just want a fresh start to put it all behind me."

Dawkins shook his head. It was as much conversation as he had ever heard Ezra make at one time. "We get out there to Washington, you'll have all kinds of chances. Timber, game, fish, ranchin', you name it." Dawkins grinned. "Got to be plenty of gals in that Seattle town."

"I ain't even been thinkin' about any of that," said Ezra. "Just want to lose that dang marshal and the army."

"I think we'll be all right if we can get out of the territory." Dawkins took a stick from the woodpile and scratched a map near the fire. "Once we get across Mullan Pass, we got a few days' ride to Missoula. Then it's on to Lolo Pass and good-bye Montana Territory." Dawkins threw the stick in the fire and drank his coffee while studying the map.

Ezra nodded to the north. "What if they keep comin'? What if they don't stop at the border?"

"Then you two ride to Canada," said Dawkins, pointing to the map. "The border is less than a hundred miles from the Idaho line."

"What about you, Bill?"

"It'll be easier for me to give 'em the slip by myself," answered Dawkins. "But I'm goin' to Seattle—"

"You bet you are." Ezra chuckled. "Like the Métis say, 'Elle est tres jolie, non?'"

Dawkins nodded and pointed toward Jim. "Better get your brother goin'. We need to eat and get moving. I'll fetch a little more wood for the breakfast fire."

Dawkins sat on a fallen log near the river. Away from the cottonwoods, the rising sun cast plenty of light, and Dawkins pulled Adel's letter from his shirt pocket. He read it again, some parts twice. He smelled the perfume that lingered on the paper.

If it were not for all this trouble, he could have joined her on the stage to Seattle. That would be good. They could share the countryside and enjoy the new sights together. Let someone else care for the horses and gear. A way station would wait at the end of every day, with a hot meal and a warm bed.

In the rush of running, Dawkins had scarcely taken in the trail. In the last throes of summer, the Missouri ran low, and wildflowers—red, orange, blue, and purple—crowded the grassy riverbanks. Willows rustled in the wind, some already bearing yellow leaves. The dusty plains gave way to rolling hills covered in a blanket of pines. To the west, the high country loomed, where jagged peaks crowned the skyline.

Of course, he chuckled, if it were not for all this trouble, there would have been no rendezvous with the *Chambers*. Adel would be headed to Seattle to marry a stranger. Dawkins and the Millers would be wandering aimlessly to the west.

Meeting Adel like that—some called it fate or chance, or maybe God's doings. Some people believed in coincidence, and

JIM SATTERFIELD

some figured life was all scripted, with things all planned out and meant to happen. Others talked about man's free will.

His mother had taken him to the little church near the farm most every Sunday. Papa stayed home, saying he was not sure. Maybe it was too soon to tell which one had rubbed off on him. But he was starting to see it Mother's way.

Chapter Twenty

Adel came to the tack room after lunch, bringing Craft a solid meal of meat and cheese sandwiches. She had let him sleep after leaving at sunrise and figured he must be awake by now.

Sure enough, when she entered the room, Craft greeted her anxiously. "Doctor, I've never been so hungry in my life. I could eat all that and more."

"Good, good," said Adel. "You haven't had anything besides soup and liquids for several days, so let's start off slow." She placed the plate of food on the bench and sat beside Craft. "How's your hand feel? Let's see."

"I'm fine, just hungry as a wolf."

Adel laughed and unwrapped the cloth strip from his hand. "Looks good, Lieutenant," she mused while examining his arm. "Your color's fine, and the swelling's still down. It will be a week or two before the wrinkled skin tightens, but that's normal." She freshened the ointment and applied a new bandage. "Now you can eat, Lieutenant."

Adel watched Craft tear into the sandwiches, hoping he would not choke. She asked, "What's next for you, Lieutenant?"

"Marshal Beidler said he'd wire Fort Keogh when we reach Fort Benton, see what the army wants to do with me." Craft took a drink of water. "I'd guess they'll have me take this steamer back to the Milk River Landing."

"You should be all healed up by then," said Adel. "Captain La Barge expects to make Fort Benton by this evening."

"What sort of man is Marshal Beidler, Lieutenant?" Adel had her own ideas, but she was curious about Craft's view.

Craft's smile disappeared. "He's a hard man. I think he's the sort that doesn't give up, once he's set his mind to something."

"Is he a fair man? Is he honest?"

Craft placed the rest of his sandwich on the plate and sat back. "I don't think fairness and honesty come into play when he's on a chase, Doctor."

Adel wondered how far she should go, what she would share with Craft. She decided he needed to hear it all. "This one fellow that you're after for attacking the guard?"

"Yes, ma'am?"

"Do you know why he attacked the soldier?"

"I just heard he didn't want his goods confiscated."

Adel took a deep breath. "The soldier killed his fiancée, that's why the man you're after beat him."

Craft turned his head to speak, but Adel went on. "Your troop had a fight with the Sioux, shortly after you took after these three men. You were fortunate not to lose your entire command. Didn't you ever wonder why the man who flanked you retreated instead of attacking from the rear?"

"Doctor, how do you know all this?" Craft's eyes widened, then he squinted and shook his head.

"Because I know the man who risked his life to protect your troop from the Sioux. He could have saved himself, but he stayed and shot two warriors before they could ride over the top of your men."

"That's why they retreated..." Craft closed his eyes and rubbed his forehead.

"You found your horses along the Missouri, along with an elk quarter," Adel said, "and when your people were ambushed below the Milk, was anyone in your command actually hit?"

"What are you telling me? Why are you telling me this?" Craft asked as he turned toward Adel with raised eyebrows.

"I thought you should know about the people you've been chasing," said Adel. "They're not outlaws, they're not bad men." Adel took a deep breath and fought to keep her composure. "Marshal Beidler nearly killed you getting you to this boat so he could catch his prey. You nearly died from blood poisoning and exhaustion, not that snake bite."

Craft sagged against his pillow.

"Do you have a girl, Lieutenant?" Adel asked. "Someone you really care for? Someone you want to spend the rest of your life with?"

Craft sat up and smiled. "Yes ma'am, Becky Brown. We met when I was at the Point, my fourth year. She promised she'd wait for me. I'm counting the days until I can send for her."

"If you give me your word of honor, Lieutenant, that this will remain between us, I'll tell you about my new love."

Craft looked Adel in the eye. "I give you my word."

"His name is Bill Dawkins, and he's one of the men you're after, or at least the marshal is now." Adel felt the cross on her chest. "He's the man who saved your command near the Milk River." Tears filled her eyes. "He's the one who stole and returned your horses and fed you in the wilderness. He didn't want to hurt either of you. He's just trying to keep the two young men he's with free. He's trying to escape the territory, and if he does, we're going to start a new life together in Seattle."

Craft dropped his head.

"I just thought you should know, Lieutenant," said Adel, wiping her eyes with a kerchief. "There's a lot more to all of this than you realize. I think the marshal is more interested in hunting men than justice or the truth." She paused. "You seem like a fine young man. In a few weeks, you'll be back with your regiment at Fort Keogh, and I hope Becky joins you soon."

Craft nodded weakly, staring across the room. "I hope so, too."

"To be a good officer, you'll need to learn about the true nature of people, not just tactics and strategy," said Adel. "That's why I thought you should know what sort of man you've been chasing…and the company you keep."

Captain La Barge moored the *Chambers* a few miles upstream of the Marias River. He hoped to reach Fort Benton early in the afternoon, but the wind had picked up, ruffling the surface and hiding snags and sawyers. La Barge was not going to get careless this close to the end of his last trip upriver.

Now they would probably arrive around nightfall, but what did a few more hours matter after steaming for six weeks? One way or another, his crew would unload the freight, take on a load for points downstream, and return to St. Louis. The journey back only took two or three weeks. Then he would settle for work closer to home.

In the meantime, he planned to enjoy his last few days on the Upper Missouri. He would spend a few days in Fort Benton, supervising the transfer of cargo and putting a good crew together for the return voyage. There would be time to visit friends in Fort Benton, maybe even spend a night or two at one of the hotels in town.

He was about to leave the pilothouse when Marshal Beidler knocked on a window and entered. La Barge did not care for the man, but had a healthy respect for his authority. La Barge had once been subpoenaed by another federal marshal, nearly losing his boat in the affair.

"Captain, I'm going to ride the rest of the way to Fort Benton," said Beidler. "We're just a few miles away now, and I need to find a telegraph and contact Marshal Piney in Helena. I'll try to reach the army at Fort Keogh about Craft."

"It sounds like the lieutenant is going to be all right, according to Dr. Johnston," said La Barge. He thought that would please Beidler, but the man hardly noticed.

"I'll come back to the *Chambers* after you make the landing at Fort Benton," said Beidler. "If the army asks, are you willing to take Craft downriver, maybe as far as the Milk?"

"Of course he can stay on."

"Well, the army will provide scrip for his voyage, as well as mine." Beidler shook his head. "It's the least they can do for the territory, sending me on this fool's errand."

Against his better judgment, La Barge asked, "Does that mean you're through chasing those hunters we took on?" La Barge was hoping he could provide Adel good news.

"Hell, no, Captain," scoffed Beidler. "I'm just gettin' started." The little man took his eye off the river and stared up at La Barge. "If I could prove that you aided those men, I'd arrest you and take you to the territorial court in Helena. I've got my suspicions, though."

"I'm sorry you feel that way, Marshal." La Barge had long since learned to hide his emotions and thoughts from bold, vindictive men like Beidler. "Without the lieutenant, I guess you'll be on your own."

Beidler laughed. "That sorry pup ain't got the sense God gave geese. I'm better off without him."

La Barge had heard enough. "Well, we'll look for you at the landing."

Beidler nodded and left the pilothouse. A few minutes later, La Barge saw him walk his mount across the gangplank to the shore. Then Beidler mounted his horse and spurred it into a gallop toward Fort Benton.

Near sundown, the *Chambers* made the Fort Benton levee. La Barge let the crew fire the cannons to announce the steamer's arrival, and soon the boat was docked along the north shore. Passengers and crew lined the railings, waving to bystanders and kin standing on the dock. From the pilothouse, La Barge viewed Front Street, cut parallel to the Missouri, with its general stores, hotels, saloons, and gambling halls. He noticed new brick buildings rising among the older wooden structures. Mountains of freight were piled here and there along the river. Everywhere lanterns flickered in the dwindling light.

La Barge left the pilothouse after the *Chambers* was moored. At the same time he reached the lower deck, the gangplanks were extended to the dock. He saw Marshal Beidler push and shove his way through the crowd along the levee and board the *Chambers*.

Beidler spared any social graces. "Captain, I got to be goin' right away," he said as he approached La Barge. He pulled a small piece of yellow paper from his pocket and handed it to the captain. "I was right, the army wants you to take Craft back down to the Milk."

"If you want to say good-bye to the lieutenant, Dr. Johnston tells me he's up and alert." La Barge pointed toward the ship's stable and tack room.

"I ain't got time for that," said Beidler, pointing to the south. "I'll be riding all night as it is. Got my orders, too, and I'm taking off for those three friends of yours."

La Barge nodded but said nothing.

Beidler grinned. "Could you pass along a message for me?"

"Of course."

"You can tell that lady doctor, Miss Johnston, there ain't gonna be any teary-eyed reunion in Seattle with that Dawkins character."

"Is that so?" La Barge raised his eyebrows but was not surprised Beidler had deduced a few facts after spending two days on the *Chambers*. He was glad to be rid of him, but he allowed himself one gratuitous swing at the runty lawman. "Marshal, let me share something with you."

Beidler paused in mid-step and turned toward La Barge.

"You're not half the man Bill Dawkins is," said La Barge with a smile. "He's got a two-day head start on you, and you'll catch him when pigs sprout wings."

Beidler froze and his eyes narrowed. He started to speak, then shook his head and bolted off the *Chambers*.

La Barge laughed loud enough for Beidler to hear. Then he turned his attention to his departing passengers.

In the fading light of her room on the hurricane deck, Adel finished packing her belongings. She had mixed emotions about leaving. She wanted to be on her way to a new career as a medical doctor. She also prayed her new life with Bill was near. But the boat held many memories: the pilothouse where she had become friends with Captain La Barge and viewed the indescribable Missouri so many evenings, the decks and bow where she had met other passengers and passed the time reading and writing, and the tack room where first she had treated Bill Dawkins as a patient and later came to know him and the Miller twins.

Adel was nearly finished when someone knocked on her door. "It's Captain La Barge, Adel," she heard him say from the walkway.

Adel opened the door and left the room. "Good evening, Captain. I'm all packed." She smiled and nodded toward her luggage.

"I'll have a man take it to your hotel. I'd be glad to walk you there myself if you would like."

"That would be wonderful, would you?"

"Certainly, I can't leave for a few minutes—"

"That would be fine, Captain," blurted Adel. "I'd like to walk around the boat a little...I need to check on Lieutenant Craft."

"Oh, yes, the lieutenant," said La Barge. "The army will be sending him downriver with us."

"That's excellent," said Adel. She could not bear the thought of the young man taking up the chase again with Beidler. "Now that marshal will be on his own."

La Barge hesitated before he spoke. "I hope someday we can all have a good laugh at that man's expense." He smiled and pointed below. "I'll meet you near the gangway." He tipped his hat and walked toward the stairs to the bottom deck.

Adel opened her door and took one last look around the small room. She took her purse from the bed and headed for the tack room and Lieutenant Craft. She felt good about Craft's prospects. His hand was almost completely healed, and he would have plenty of time to rest on the return voyage. She sensed that he had learned a lot about soldiering and people since leaving West Point in the spring. Rounding the walkway to the tack room, she thought she would give him her address in Seattle so she could learn about the trip downriver and his future plans.

When she entered the room, now nearly dark, Lieutenant Craft was gone.

Beidler rode as fast as he dared along Benton Road. Only a half moon lit the winding wagon trail, but he figured he could reach Mullan Pass blindfolded. Over the years, he had made the trip between Helena and Fort Benton at least a hundred times. He gave the roan mare her head, and she ran hard for him in the cool night air. He held the reins with his left hand and pulled along a second horse with his right. Sometime around first light, when the mare played out or died, he would swap horses and keep riding.

After Beidler had reached Fort Benton in late afternoon, he went directly to the military post on the edge of town. He explained his business with the post commander, a graying major by the name of Ilges. The major offered no men to assist Beidler, saying his small detachment could barely muster a daily guard. Major Ilges lent him a second mount and allowed him to use the post's telegraph.

He quickly received a response from Fort Keogh, instructing him to send Craft downriver on the *Chambers*. The second response from Helena took longer, and Beidler walked about the post impatiently for over an hour before the corporal emerged from headquarters with a yellow slip of paper. Marshal Piney ordered Beidler to continue his pursuit of the three fugitives as he saw fit and practicable. However, Piney admonished Beidler not to cross the territory border under any circumstances. Out of hearing from the corporal or other soldiers, Beidler cursed and stuffed the note in his shirt pocket.

Now he rode in darkness, wondering how to catch this fellow Dawkins and the Miller twins. They had two days' head start, but Beidler knew some shortcuts along the way. He could use his authority to requisition fresh horses and food from the stage lines, stopping only enough to sleep a few hours here and there. With a little luck he would catch up with the three men before they reached the border. If Dawkins and the Millers reached Idaho, Beidler was already working on an excuse for crossing the border.

Chapter Twenty-one

When Dawkins and the Millers came to a fork in the Benton Road, they headed west for Mullan Pass. They had been on the trail since sunrise, and now the mid-August sun reminded them summer still had plenty of fight left. Without pulling his watch, the keepsake given to him by Adel, Dawkins figured it was close to noon. They passed through a treeless valley surrounded by pine-covered hills interspersed with tawny parks. Dawkins saw Threemile Creek ahead and planned to water the horses and let the boys rest awhile.

Dawkins looked over his shoulder at the Millers. Like him, they rode in quiet determination. Even Jim had stopped joking about fooling Beidler and being the next Jesse James. By the time they reached Idaho, they would have crossed nearly the entire Montana Territory. It was a long way to be chased, and Dawkins saw wear on the young men. They looked gaunt even though they ate their fill of venison and biscuits and whatever else he could scrape up every night. Darkness ringed their eyes, like a couple of old raccoons, and both boys had a faraway stare, like the men he had fought with in Pennsylvania and Virginia.

Dawkins was hanging tough. He liked to idle the time away, thinking about Adel and Washington Territory. Adel had told him what to expect from the paintings and pictures she had studied back East. In his mind, he had already built the house he would raise for her. He hoped to find a quiet ridge near town, with a view of the Pacific and the snow-clad peaks of the Cascade Range.

Funny thing, the farther they traveled from Fort Benton and the closer they were to freedom, the more anxious and worried he became. He had taken to studying their back trail again, especially in this open country where a man could see for miles with field glasses. More than once, he spied a group of riders raising dust and heading their way. Dawkins kept watching the strangers until he identified them as a stage or another band of travelers. Once, he even pulled the boys off the trail and into timber to let strangers pass, a bunch of nameless wanderers.

Finally, Threemile Creek loomed near, and Dawkins let his mount trot toward the smell of water and lush grass. They rode off the trail and down into a small draw where a thick stand of willows and cottonwoods stood. Dawkins heard the creek before he saw it. A noisy little stream, it still bore snow-melt from the Continental Divide, and in some places a man could jump across its reach. In the shade, the water looked green with blue pockets where the sun peeked through the overhanging trees. Dawkins and the boys dismounted and let their horses drink.

"Good to get out of that sun," said Jim. He filled his hat from the stream and poured the creek water on his head. "Whew, that feels good."

Ezra followed his brother's lead, and Dawkins laughed. "Better do that twice, 'cause there's not much shade along the way."

"How far we got, Bill, to the pass?" asked Ezra.

"Maybe ten miles," said Dawkins. He loosened his horse's cinch and tied the mare to a short cottonwood. "Let's sit a spell."

Jim sat and chewed on a long stem of grass. "Feels good here in the shade, but I know we ought to be ridin'."

"We'll go soon enough, but we got some business to iron out first," said Dawkins. He paused and eyed the twins. No matter how sweet life with Adel might be, things would never be right if he did not look after them first.

"By now, Beidler's well past Fort Benton. Don't know if he wired ahead, got help at the Fort, or if he's just comin' himself."

"We just got to keep movin'," said Jim.

"Directly," answered Dawkins. "But first, I want your oaths on something." He took a deep breath. "Don't know when or from what direction trouble might be comin' from now. Could be behind us or even ahead. Might not be much time for figurin' if it does come."

Jim nodded. "So we'll just take things head-on."

Dawkins shook his head. "We get close to a tussle, I want you both to light out to the north. Don't stop 'til you cross the border. Where we're going, it won't be far." Jim started to speak, but Dawkins raised his hand and cut him off. "Beidler probably ain't supposed to leave the territory, but that don't mean he won't. And the army, they can go anywhere they please. That's why Canada's the safe bet for both of you."

"We ain't runnin' out on you, Bill," said Ezra as he stood and headed for the horses.

"I hope it won't come to that, but I want your word—both of you—you'll run if I say so." He was proud they hesitated, but he pressed the point. "We got the gear divided up pretty well, and I'm fixin' to split up the money Captain La Barge gave us for the hides. That'll give you a good stake."

"What about you, Bill?" Jim rose and stretched.

"I'll slow down Beidler and whoever else comes along, then I'll give 'em the slip and head for Washington." Dawkins stood and pointed north. "If you have to go up there, head west and write to Adel. I'll give you the address. I'll let you know when you can come back."

After three hours of steady riding under a cloudless sky, they reached the summit of Mullan Pass. The trail ran due west until they came to a long switchback that ended at a wide bench. Dawkins, riding in the lead, stopped and waited for Jim and Ezra to come up beside him. "We're crossing the Great Divide, boys." He pointed to the direction from which they had come. "All the streams on that side of the divide run to the Atlantic," he turned in his saddle, "and all the water yonder runs to the Pacific."

"Looks like it's all downhill from here, Bill," said Jim. He stood in his saddle, staring to the west.

"Pretty much, at least until we cross the Bitterroot Mountains," said Dawkins. "First, though, we got about eighty miles to Missoula, and another forty or so to Lolo Pass."

"Whew, boy, that's a lot of ridin'," said Jim, "but we got to keep movin'."

Dawkins ran the numbers through his mind. "Three, maybe four days at the most, if we don't run into any weather." He pointed west. "Let's move off this saddle and git. Ought to be able to reach the Hell Gate River by nightfall."

They trotted their string down the west side of Mullan Pass. Afternoon clouds cooled the ride, and they made good time. When they came around a bend in the road, they nearly ran into a freight train of over two hundred mules and a dozen wagons. Dawkins rode up a little knoll to the side of the road and let the train pass. Jim and Ezra followed, and the three men drank from their canteens as the procession of mule-drawn wagons snaked up the pass.

"Dang, them wagons got to be ten feet tall," said Jim, "and they're pulling 'em in tandem."

"They got stoves, furniture, barrels of beer, everything under the sun in those carts," said Dawkins. "Probably got a billiards table, too."

Both boys laughed, then Dawkins pointed toward a rider headed their way, saying quietly, "Let me do the talking."

A bearded man about Dawkins's age came up along the side of the train and spurred his horse up the side of the hill. He stopped a few yards below Dawkins and the Millers. "Afternoon, men." He removed his broad-brimmed hat and wiped his balding head. "Mighty hot today."

Dawkins nodded, "Howdy, that it is."

"Name's Horace Clark, I'm the freighter boss of this here train."

Dawkins thought for a moment of providing aliases to the man for himself and the boys, but he thought better of it and just nodded with a smile instead.

After a moment of awkward silence, Clark said, "Had us a bad accident this morning. One of my drivers jackknifed his team and dumped the whole rig off a three-hundred-foot drop into the Hell Gate. Two men were killed."

"Sorry to hear it." Dawkins shook his head and looked ahead where the end of the train was nearing.

"Any rate," said Clark, "I'm short-handed now, lookin' for help."

"Appreciate you mentioning it," said Dawkins, "but we're headed down to Fort Owen." It was a lie, but maybe it would throw off anyone who happened to run into this fellow.

By now the train had passed, and Dawkins motioned for the Millers to follow as he rode off the knoll. He turned back toward Clark. "Hope you have better luck the rest of the way."

In the last bit of the late summer evening, they reached the Hell Gate River. The wagon road ran along the north shore, between the river and the base of steep rock and pine-strewn hills. Dawkins found a flat piece of ground and slipped off his mount. "We must have made fifty miles today." He patted his horse and wondered how long they could keep up this pace.

Jim jumped from his horse like the youngster he was and pointed upstream. "How far to Missoula?"

"Maybe seventy miles," answered Dawkins. "Be there in a couple of days."

"Reckon we'll be needin' any fixin's by then?" asked Jim.

Ezra walked up, shaking his head. "Let's water these horses and make camp."

Dawkins was glad for Ezra's help. Sometimes Jim was too sociable for his own good. But could Ezra look after him if they had to ride to Canada?

"Jim, I don't know about stopping at Missoula, but I did buy this snakebite medicine on the *Chambers*. I think we've earned a snort." Dawkins pulled a bottle of whiskey, wrapped in an extra shirt, from his saddlebag.

Both boys hollered, and Dawkins raised a hand toward them. "This is for after we got a camp."

Within half an hour they had the horses picketed on a good patch of streamside grass. They built a fire with driftwood Ezra found along the river. Dawkins fetched the bottle and passed it around to Jim and Ezra. It was the first liquor

Dawkins had allowed himself in days, and it went straight to his head. He decided to give up the fear of being chased, at least for one night. He would have them moving again at first light. Getting Jim a little liquored up might take the sting out of passing around Missoula in the dark. No way Dawkins was going to risk stopping in any town, not until they were well out of the territory.

The boys' laughter and jabbering faded in the distance, along with the river, as Dawkins lay on his back and stared into the coal-black sky. In a while, the moon would rise, shining silver on the Hell Gate. The fire felt good in the night air, cooled by the running river. Dawkins wondered if his run was nearly done. Since he had come up to Montana Territory in '64, he had been chasing his own tail like some fool dog. Meat hunting, prospecting, hide hunting, freighting—he had tried it all. He always managed to get by, but never really ahead. What would it be like to stay in one place, work at one job?

When he first came upriver, fifteen years before, he was not fit for any woman's company. He had nightmares and memories of that war that would not let him be. Sometimes when he was feeling good and right while hunting or exploring new country, dread and sadness snuck upon him and blanketed him in despair. He might be sleeping and awake from a horrid dream, drenched in sweat. Gradually, over the months and years, the melancholy and nervousness faded away.

Now he thought he could be a husband for Adel. He would look after her, keep her from working herself to a fray caring for others, as he knew she might. She was something: smart, pretty, sweet, and tough.

Anyways, by the time they made the coast, he might never want to see the trail again. So he breathed the damp river air and listened to Jim and Ezra laughing in the night.

In a dream, Dawkins walked along the coast in the early morning light. Fog shrouded the Pacific, but he heard waves breaking along the rock-strewn beach and gulls crying overhead. He left the lush hillside and dropped down to the seashore.

When he came upon footprints in the sand, he followed, peering into the soupy mist. After a while, he called, "Adel," and stopped to listen for her response. Over the ocean's growl, he thought he heard her call his name. Her voice was soft and distant, so he took up her trail once more.

Through the morning, he walked alone, calling for her. Once, he swore he saw her, moving like a shadow, just beyond the curtain of fog. By sunrise, he was tired and rested on the beach, just above the reach of tumbling waves.

When Dawkins awoke, it was dark and he heard the Hell Gate lapping against the shore. He slipped on his boots and built a fire. He let the Millers sleep a bit longer while he inspected the horses and readied for another hard day.

Chapter Twenty-two

Beidler thought he would allow himself a couple of hours of sleep when he reached the shaded stream bottom, just a mile ahead. He urged his horse to lope and pulled along a second mount. In the midday heat, both animals were covered in a white lather and needed water.

In less than two days, Beidler had made over one hundred miles. Riding alone, hell-bent on catching these outlaws, he had often thought back to his days as a Pony Express messenger. Before he came to the territory and before he put on the gut of a middle-aged man, he rode a stretch of the route between Colorado and Wyoming. He learned to ride ten hours straight at a dead run, sometimes covering a hundred miles in a day. Every ten miles or so, about as far as a horse could run at a gallop, he would swap mounts at a relay station.

The horses on this chase were not as fortunate as the Pony Express stock. Beidler rode furiously his first night out of Fort Benton. By dawn, his horse, the one provided to him by Major Ilges, was nearly dead on its feet. When it foundered, Beidler managed to uncinch his saddle and lead the exhausted animal off the wagon road before it collapsed into a helpless pile. In the narrow confines of the canyon, Beidler's pistol sounded like a cannon fired in church. He saddled his other horse and rode hard into the morning.

By noon, he reached a way station near the Sun River. He swapped his played-out horse for a fresh mount and provided government scrip for a second. At first the stationmaster resisted, but when Beidler told the old man his business and who he was, the grizzled hand shrugged his shoulders and turned away. Beidler rode through stifling heat to the Dearborn station, another thirty miles, switching horses every ten miles or so. Once again, he traded for two more fresh mounts and rode until he came to where Mullan trail left the Benton Road.

He camped along a trickle of a stream in the Scratch Gravel Hills. He went easier on his horses, as he might not be able to trade for fresh animals until he was well beyond Mullan Pass. He figured he must have gained ground on Dawkins and those boys. No way they could match his pace.

He was on the trail again before first light. He had not slept well, missing the whiskey he had deprived himself of to save weight. He made fine time until he nearly collided with an enormous mule freight train. He fumed as the pokey mules wound their way along the narrow road. Unable to do anything but wait for them to pass, he rested his horses along a side hill. After a little while, a man with a long beard and dark eyes rode near. When the stranger saw Beidler's badge, he introduced himself as the freighter boss and apologized for the delay.

Anxious for any leads, Beidler questioned the man and learned three riders passed the train the afternoon before. They had to be his outlaws, figured Beidler. How many threesomes—that included twin brothers—could there be in this country? The freighter, a man by the name of Clark, told Beidler the men had passed on his offer of employment, saying

THE RIVER'S SONG

they were headed to Fort Owen. Clark also thought it odd they had allowed no names in introduction.

Now, as Beidler neared Threemile Creek, he once again felt the lovely thrill of the chase. He was getting near. Dawkins and the Millers could not be more than twenty miles away. He would rest and water his horses just enough to keep them running. The last ten miles to the top of the pass were tough, but then he would have a downhill run all the way to the Hell Gate River.

Near dark, Beidler discovered the outlaws' campsite from the day before. On a grassy flat above the Hell Gate River, he retraced their footsteps and studied their horses' tracks. He stumbled upon an empty whiskey bottle, and savored the few remaining drops before he tossed it in the river.

His two horses were weary, having covered twenty miles since midday. He watered them and let them graze near the same ground Dawkins and his boys had chosen for their mounts. He had no choice but to rest them, with the nearest source of remounts at least thirty miles away. He needed a few hours of sleep as well to ready himself for the last leg of his pursuit.

While picketing his horses and making a hasty camp, Beidler took stock of the situation. Since leaving Fort Benton, he had ridden around a hundred and forty miles. He killed one horse and rode two others so hard they might never recover, but that was part of the price of apprehending criminals. He hoped these men would be so bold as to spend another night in camp.

Since Beidler had taken up this trail, he had wondered about what sort of men he was chasing. He assumed it was the older one, Dawkins, who was handy with a rifle. Between the ambush where he had scurried Craft's squadron like so many rabbits and his guarding of the soldiers' flank against the Sioux, Beidler grudgingly admired the man's grit. Beidler clenched his fists, though, as he remembered how the two men had stolen his and Craft's horses in the Larb Hills. He assumed Dawkins was the man who had spoken to him at gunpoint, disarming him and leaving him afoot. In the dark with a Colt stuck in his face, Beidler had not gotten a good look at Dawkins, but he would remember the voice.

He thought of Craft for a moment. Perhaps his snakebite was a good piece of luck. If that fool greenhorn had not been struck by a rattler, Beidler would still be wet-nursing him now. Craft could never keep up the pace Beidler had set for himself over the last two days. If not for Craft's misfortune, Beidler might not have learned of Dawkins's plan to rendezvous with the lady doctor in Seattle. Maybe the army could find something for that boy to do, like building bridges or whatever it was he had learned at West Point. But he was sure not cut out for the field. The kid was lucky Beidler had been willing to drag him along to the Missouri and find a doctor on that steamer.

Beidler had learned a lot about the outlaws during the two days he spent on the *Chambers*. Besides names and physical descriptions of the men, he figured he had put nearly all the pieces of the puzzle together. To win that lady doctor's affection, Dawkins must be more than just another hand with a rifle and a horse. He was probably educated and well spoken. Charming, some folks would say. Then there were the two young men, not even kin, that he was leading. Those boys might be his weakness. A man who had risked his neck to protect his own pursuers from the Sioux would probably sacrifice himself to protect two young men in his charge.

THE RIVER'S SONG

Beidler realized it was Dawkins he wanted. That was his quarry, not a couple of pups along for the ride. The army might be more interested in whichever of the twins had beaten the soldier along Rock Creek, but not Beidler. Dawkins was the challenge and the trophy he sought. Beidler did not know how many more hunts he had left in him after this trek across most of Montana Territory. Over the long days on horseback and afoot, surely he had left part of himself on the trail. Catching Dawkins would make it all worthwhile.

For the first time in days, Beidler slept deeply in his bare camp along the Hell Gate. Perhaps it was the soothing rhythm of the river, or maybe just exhaustion from so many long miles on the trail. But when he arose near midnight to make water, he was sorely tempted to return to his bedroll and sleep until dawn.

He mustered all his will to add wood to the fire and prepare to travel. He allowed himself the luxury of coffee, filling his battered enamel pot from the river and placing it on a flat rock by the fire. Waiting for the water to boil, he ate some dried beef and crackers from the stores at Fort Benton. He rolled up his bedroll and packed what little gear he had into his saddlebags. When the pot steamed, he threw in a handful of grounds and let it cool while he saddled one of the horses.

The river bottom was cold and dewy. He sat on a log and drank his first cup of coffee while he shivered inside his coat. The strong brew braced him, and shortly he was glad he had not succumbed to the lure of a warm bed. He remembered a rhyme he had heard as a young man when he rode for the Pony Express, "Awake, awake, awake you knave, there'll be time to sleep when you're in the grave."

He rose from his seat along the river and tossed the last dregs of coffee from his cup on the ground. He emptied his pot on the fire, and steam rose, white in the moonlight. He packed his pot and cup into his saddlebags and walked over to his horses, still picketed along the riverbank. After tying his saddlebags and bedroll to his saddle, he pulled his rifle from its scabbard and checked its load.

He had left behind his trusty shotgun at Fort Benton, preferring the loan of a cavalry carbine for the work ahead. Long-range work, where he could show off his own shooting prowess.

Stiffly, Beidler mounted up and led his horse across the gravelly flat to the wagon trail, jerking along the second animal, still balky from rest. When his little string made the road, he headed them west at a trot. After his horse settled into its gait, Beidler spurred it harshly, and they galloped along the moonlit river.

Chapter Twenty-three

Dawkins climbed a few hundred feet to a bench overlooking the Bitterroot River, where it finished its northerly run to the Hell Gate. In the growing light, Dawkins sat on a flat rock, scanning the enormous basin before him. To his left, lights twinkled in Missoula, and he viewed a maze of timbered ridges, valleys, and streams to the east. He slowly examined the wagon trail running along the Bitterroot, all the way to where it meandered out of sight west of town, ten miles away.

After two long days of riding along the Hell Gate River, he and the Millers had reached the edge of Missoula the evening before. Dawkins led Jim and Ezra around the east side of town, crossing the Hell Gate on a newly built bridge. A few miles later, they crossed the Bitterroot and followed the wagon road to where it met the Lolo Trail. They rode a few hundred yards along Lolo Creek and camped on the valley bottom.

The Idaho Territory border loomed less than thirty miles to the west. Dawkins knew the trail had been well cleared a couple of years before when Chief Joseph and his people led the US Army on a chase almost all the way to Canada. In his pursuit of the Nez Perce, General Howard employed fifty ax men to clear deadfall along the trail. Dawkins had heard that between the Indians and the soldiers, four or five thousand horses had beaten a path through the rocky, timbered country.

Dawkins had never traveled the Lolo, but he remembered reading about the war in the *Helena Independent*. The first ten miles was easy, but if he remembered correctly, it was tough up-and-down going after that.

One hard day and they would be free. They could mosey across northern Idaho to Lewiston and then ride southwest to Fort Walla Walla. With a little luck, he might still get to share some of that stagecoach ride to Seattle with Adel.

Dawkins stopped his daydreaming and scanned the valley below. He saw wagons about, hauling lumber and hay, and men riding along the trails and roads south of Missoula. Deer emerged in the meadows along the Bitterroot, shining red in the morning sun. Somewhere behind him, an elk bugled in the foothills below. It looked to be another cloudless day, at least until afternoon. Maybe hot, but good traveling weather, with little chance of rain to muck up the trail and slow their escape.

Dawkins decided to scan the basin once more before climbing down the mountainside to camp. When he left before first light, he roused the Millers and figured they should have camp packed and the string readied by now. Viewing the river road, Dawkins saw the first sign of trouble. Just south of the where the Bitterroot joined the Hell Gate, two horses raised a trail of dust. Even from where Dawkins sat, at least five miles away, he could tell the riders were coming at a gallop. Dawkins noticed the second rider was mighty close to the first. Then he realized there was only one horseman leading a second mount.

Dawkins rose and ran down the steep hillside to camp. He tripped once and nearly fell on the rocky slope. Limbs and branches pulled at his arms and scratched his face, but he kept his pace until reaching the valley floor. Running through a thin stand of aspen, he glimpsed smoke rising from camp, and then he saw Jim and Ezra waiting with the horses, all saddled and packed.

"We got to move. He's comin'. Can't be too far now," Dawkins shouted with what little wind he had left. He reached the Millers and pointed down the valley to the east. He saw the look of disbelief on the boys' faces, wide-eyed and questioning.

"What'd ya see? What'd ya see?" asked Jim impatiently while Dawkins hunched over, hands on his knees, gasping for air.

Dawkins straightened and nodded toward the Bitterroot. "Beidler's comin'. I saw him from up on the ridge." He took a couple of deep breaths. "Can't be more than two or three miles away now." Dawkins shook his head. "He's leadin' a second horse, too."

Ezra cursed softly while Jim kicked the ground and shook his head.

"I know, I know," said Dawkins with a weak smile. "I was thinkin', prayin', we were done with him. But that's Beidler, I'm sure of it."

Dawkins had hoped there would be more time for good-byes. Shoot, he had hoped there would be no good-byes, but here they were. "You boys got to go, right now." Before either brother could argue, he raised his hand and tilted his head. "Remember, you gave me your word, both of you."

Dawkins rushed to both of them, and they huddled in a close embrace. He stepped back and felt a lump in his throat. He chuckled as he fought back tears. "You two mount up and git. I'll hold off Beidler as long as I can."

Ezra rubbed his eyes. "Don't let him get you, Bill." He climbed his horse and took the lead for the pack string from Jim.

"We'll be along in the fall to see you and the missus," said Jim with a laugh. He mounted his horse and smiled. "See ya in Seattle!"

Jim scooted his horse past Ezra and headed up the valley at a trot. Ezra turned in his saddle toward Dawkins. "I'll do my best to keep him out of trouble."

"You two need to look out for each other." Dawkins smiled.

Ezra nodded and took off after Jim, tugging at the pack string. Soon he caught up with his brother, and they faded into a cloud of dust.

Dawkins mounted his own horse and rushed down valley to intercept Beidler before he reached the head of the Lolo Trail. Dawkins needed time to find the right place to ambush the lawman. He had done it before on the Milk River, and he could do it again.

Beidler left the river road a few miles north of the Lolo trailhead. He cut across a bend in the Bitterroot, riding along the base of the mountainside. He had planned to ride up Lolo canyon before first light but was unable to keep the murderous pace through the night he had managed most of the day before. Finding fresh mounts was not as easy as along Benton Road, so he limped into Missoula with worn-out horses. He requisitioned two more at a way station on the edge of town, intimidating the stage master after dragging the poor man out of bed in the middle of the night.

Now the sun was well above the mountains to the east, and Beidler was wary of riding into another one of Dawkins's ambushes. Beidler was as certain as he could be the man was near. He had a hunch Dawkins would employ another rearguard maneuver as he had below the Milk weeks ago. He had probably sent those two boys on up the trail toward Idaho and points beyond. That was fine with Beidler. He was after Dawkins, not those whelps.

A few miles before the Bitterroot wagon trail forked off to the Lolo, Beidler left the road and headed west, up Deadman Gulch. He rode hard on the steep incline for a couple of miles. Then he came to another road that ran another three miles south to Lolo Creek. If Dawkins was waiting for him at the trailhead, Beidler had him cut off from heading up the Lolo.

Riding down the mountain trail, Beidler planned his own ambush. He would tie his horses a few hundred yards from the trail and walk down to the valley floor. He needed to find a spot that commanded a good view of the creek bottom within rifle range of any riders traveling up the trail.

After two hours of riding on tough mountain trails, Beidler reached the vantage point he sought, at the edge of the timber bordering Lolo. He sat on damp leaves, resting his rifle over a fallen log that broke up his silhouette. From the impromptu blind, he could see across the narrow valley to the north bank of Lolo Creek. Downstream, to the east, he viewed at least a mile of meadow.

It was a good spot, Beidler figured, and he settled in for a wait. Checking his watch, he resolved to remain for at least a couple of hours. He drank from his canteen and uncased his field glasses. He had a good feeling, a lawman's hunch that his hunt was nearly over.

Dawkins waited in the timber near the mouth of the valley. From his hiding place, he saw the Bitterroot across a wide meadow and a good piece of the wagon trail. The road disappeared from view about two miles to the north, where it followed a westward bend in the river.

He rushed to the spot right after sending Jim and Ezra on their way up the trail. Relieved to reach a good ambush point before Beidler appeared on the road, Dawkins concealed his horses in the pines to the rear and readied his Sharps. Expecting Beidler to appear at any moment, Dawkins wrestled with his conscience over how to stop the relentless lawman. He considered shooting Beidler's horses, but unless he broke his neck in the fall, the determined lawman would just remount and pick up the trail again. Dawkins was unsure if he could really shoot a United States Deputy Marshal.

After more than three hours of waiting, Dawkins wondered where Beidler had gone. At the pace Dawkins had seen him riding, the lawman should have long since reached the turnoff to Lolo Creek. Dawkins rested the Sharps in his shooting sticks and rubbed his forehead. Then a thought ran through Dawkins's mind that left him with a chill. What if Beidler knew a way to cut across the ridge to the south and come into the valley from above him?

Dawkins checked the time once more and decided to move. He slipped back to where his horses were tied and mounted up. The timber along the edge of the valley was too thick to travel through, so he crossed the trail and rode along the creek. His path was as distant from the north edge of the valley as it could be, offering anyone trying to dry-gulch him the longest shot possible.

Dawkins moved up the valley, first walking and then at a canter. He looked ahead where the narrow meadow veered to the left. When he reached that point, around a mile away, he would feel better. Something told him to move faster, make himself a tougher target. He nudged his mount into a gallop, pulling along the packhorse.

As the wind rushed across his face, Dawkins realized he was nearly played out from weeks of running. If he were fresh and thinking straight, maybe he would not have exposed himself so badly in this open valley. He could have waited in the timber until dark, and then slipped out of sight. Maybe, but then again, Beidler might have reached Jim and Ezra. Dawkins wondered if he had lost his patience and caution in his rush to reach Adel. He wanted to be with her so bad he ached with loneliness. Right or wrong, he was committed now, so he urged his horse to run and leaned forward to provide as small a target as he could.

Beidler heard the rider coming before he saw him. Down valley, to his left, the unmistakable sound of hooves in flight came to him. He rose to one knee and used his field glasses to locate the horses. Across the valley, near the creek he saw one horse, and then another, still a mile away. He looked across the meadow and estimated his shot would be at least a quarter of a mile when the riders passed. Too far, thought Beidler. He slipped from behind the log and crawled toward the creek on hands and knees, using the foot-high grass to conceal himself.

By the time he cut the distance to the far side of the valley by half, the riders were only a few hundred yards away. Beidler sat in a patch of deep grass and watched the horses approach at a dead run. He saw there was only one man pulling along a second packhorse. Just as he had calculated, Beidler chuckled, the outlaw had sent the boys ahead. Beidler cocked the Springfield carbine and took a sitting position, with his elbows resting on his knees. He found the front horse in the sights and tracked his target as it neared.

Nearing the turn in the meadow, Dawkins urged his horse to keep its pace. Out of the corner of his eye, he saw a bright flash, and an instant later, a thunderous roar came from the right. A plume of smoke rose from the grass, and then he felt his horse stumble. A splotch of blood blossomed on its neck, and its front legs buckled. Dawkins was thrown from the saddle, and he flew toward the ground. He raised his arms to break the fall, and the world exploded in blinding light, followed by silent darkness.

Chapter Twenty-four

In the gloom of dusk, Dawkins awoke to the sound of a crackling campfire. He shook his head and twisted his face to clear the fog from his mind. When he tried to rub the sleep from his eyes, his hands came up short, and he heard the unmistakable clink of chain links. He was handcuffed to the pine tree next to him.

"Welcome back to the livin'," spoke a voice from across the fire. A short man wearing a broad felt hat and a silver badge came near. "Pleased to meet you, Dawkins. I'm US Deputy Marshal John X. Beidler." He tipped his hat in mock formality.

Dawkins looked up at the famous vigilante-turned-lawman and hung his head.

"Aw, I was hopin' you'd be more sociable, hoss," said Beidler, rubbing his bushy mustache. "I've been chasin' ya so long, I almost feel like we're kin." He knelt next to Dawkins and chuckled. "I guess you don't feel quite as bold now as you did the last time we spoke."

Dawkins raised his head and gave Beidler a questioning look.

"You remember, don't you? When you stuck a gun in my face and stole my horses along Willow Creek."

"I remember."

"Good, good," said Beidler. He pointed toward Dawkins's hands. "I hope them cuffs ain't too tight."

"They're all right."

Beidler returned to his seat by the fire. "I've been waitin' all afternoon to visit with you. I'm mighty glad you woke."

Slowly but surely, Dawkins regained his wits. He remembered his horse being shot and taking a bad fall. After that, everything was a blank.

"I've been goin' through your things, Bill." Beidler smiled maliciously. "You don't mind if I call you Bill, do you? You can call me X."

Dawkins sat up and leaned against the tree.

"Anyways, I found some interesting things." Beidler lifted Dawkins's saddlebags and placed them across the fallen log where he sat. He opened one of the bags and removed a letter. "This is some doin's, now, this is…" Beidler scanned the first page of Adel's writing and chuckled. "Mercy." He read on for a bit then fanned himself with the paper. "Oh, my…"

Dawkins saw his future, and it did not look good. Beidler baiting and mocking him until the pint-sized lawman delivered him to a judge and a damp and dingy jail. He could hardly stand to watch Beidler touch, let alone read, Adel's letter.

Beidler looked at Dawkins. "Listen to this part. She says here that she'll keep you warm during—"

"I know what it says," Dawkins snapped.

Beidler jerked his head toward Dawkins and squeezed the pages of the letter in his fist. He tossed the ball of paper into the fire. Dawkins watched it burn yellow, then green and blue.

"She's a good-lookin' woman, Bill. Wonder what she'll look like in fifteen, twenty years?"

Dawkins figured she would look mighty fine, but he knew what Beidler was driving at.

"Because that's about how long I reckon they'll give you at Red Lodge." Beidler smiled. "Now, if it was up to me, I'd vote for a hangin', but I doubt they'll go that far with you." He chuckled. "Maybe she'll wait for you."

Dawkins leaned against the pine. "Maybe."

"Bull," scoffed Beidler. "Sporty thing like that? Once she figures you ain't coming out there, she'll forget about you faster than—"

"Marshal, ain't you had enough?" asked Dawkins.

"I'll tell you what it is, Bill," said Beidler. "You just get down on your knees, sir, and pray for forgiveness, and maybe the Lord will forgive you. But I sure won't. I walked my tail off for thirty miles on account of you. Rode across half the territory, to boot. So I'll let you know when I've had enough."

Dawkins shivered through the night, sleeping on and off in the cold while suffering a splitting headache from his fall. With only a sweaty saddle blanket for bedding, he awoke in the early hours of morning after the fire died out. He heard Beidler snore in the dark, and after a while Dawkins made out his form across the fire.

Dawkins tested the handcuffs about his wrists. They were loose enough to provide circulation to his hands, but he was not about to wriggle out of them. He looked up and examined the pine to which he was secured. It was only nine or ten inches across but tall, with lots of sweeping branches. He was not getting out of this camp tonight, he thought.

With Beidler asleep, Dawkins wriggled his hips toward the tree and checked his pockets. He was relieved to feel the bulge of the watch Adel had given him. Now that her letter was gone, it was his only keepsake. Yet he still had her memory etched in his mind. And he still remembered every word she had written him. He tried not to despair, figuring it was a long way back to Helena, where he supposed Beidler would haul him. One mistake on the marshal's part, he thought, and he would seize the chance to escape. In the meantime, he would play it smart and try to lull Beidler into a false sense of security.

Dawkins was surprised when Beidler rose well before sunrise and added wood to the fire. He ambled over to the brush surrounding camp and relieved himself. Then he rummaged through his saddlebags and found a coffeepot. Dawkins heard water gurgle from a canteen.

"You up, Dawkins?" Beidler asked in a hoarse voice. "We're gonna be moving soon, so you need to be risin' now."

"I'm up already, just lyin' here, Marshal."

"Didn't sleep too well, did ya?"

"Can't complain," lied Dawkins.

Beidler stoked the fire, casting light about the camp. He knelt near Dawkins, key to the cuffs in hand. "Bill, now that you're clearheaded, let me tell you how our partnership is gonna work." Beidler handed him the key and then unholstered his Colt. "Long as you don't make no trouble for me, like tryin' to escape or the like, I'll treat you fair. I'll share whatever grub and water I got, and I might even let you have your bedroll for sleepin'." He waved his pistol at Dawkins. "But the first time you pull somethin', I'll cut your food and water to just enough to keep you alive for the court. You understand me?"

Dawkins nodded.

"Say it."

"I understand, Marshal."

"All right, then unlock them cuffs from around that tree, and then lock 'em back on. You can go make water directly."

Beidler rose and pointed his pistol at Dawkins. "I been haulin' around outlaws for nearly twenty years. You best behave yourself and forget about escaping."

Dawkins followed the marshal's orders and placed the key on the ground.

Throughout the early morning, Beidler never gave Dawkins any opening. They ate a scant breakfast of dried meat, hardtack, and coffee. Beidler locked him to the tree again and then packed their gear and readied the horses.

Just after sunrise, they left camp, heading back down the Lolo trail toward the Bitterroot. Dawkins rode Beidler's spare horse with the handcuffs run through the saddle's pommel and his second horse tied onto the tail of his mount. Beidler led the way, tugging at the reins of Dawkins's horse. "You better hope I don't take a fall," hollered Beidler from the front of the little caravan. 'Cause you ain't goin' nowhere, cuffed to that horse and towing along the pack animal. Best just settle in for the ride."

By midday they reached the southern edge of Missoula. Dawkins was not surprised when Beidler swiveled on his mount. "I could leave you here or maybe get another man to go along with us, but I think I'll just take you to Helena myself." Beidler laughed. "Besides, we can talk some more tonight."

Riding through the outskirts of town along the Bitterroot and across the Hell Gate Bridge, Dawkins felt like Beidler's trophy. The tiny lawman puffed up like some old bullfrog every time folks passed. He would tip his hat or nod his head and then glance over his shoulder toward Dawkins. "Taking a wanted man to territorial court," Beidler boasted.

Dawkins dropped his head and shunned the attention people gave him. He could scarcely wait to reach the edge of town, although it was awful disheartening to cover the same ground he and the Millers had ridden only the day before. The same ground, all right, but in the wrong direction. Heading west, every step had felt that much closer to freedom and Adel. Now he was nearing a penitentiary with each passing mile. Beidler was savvy about handling a prisoner, too. Dawkins figured they had four or five more days on the trail before reaching Helena. He would not give up, but with a lawman like Beidler, the chances of escaping did not look good.

Well before sundown, Beidler halted his horse and pointed toward a grassy flat off the Hell Gate wagon road. "We'll camp yonder, along the timber."

Once again, he held Dawkins at gunpoint and handed over the keys to the handcuffs. "Uncuff yourself from that saddle and get off your horse." Beidler marched Dawkins to a middling-sized poplar and watched him lock himself to the trunk. "You just wait there, and I'll take care of the horses and make us a camp."

By sundown, Beidler had the stock picketed on lush grass and a fire going near the edge of timber that ran up the mountainside behind them. "I checked your saddlebags, Dawkins. How come you ain't carrying no liquor for the trail?"

Dawkins did not see the harm in gabbing a little with the marshal. Maybe he would give him a bedroll. "We had us a bottle, but we drank it all along the Hell Gate, maybe fifty miles to the east."

"Yeah, I found that camp." Beidler grinned and rubbed his hands by the fire. "How 'bout them two boys you been ridin' with, the Millers? Why don't you reckon they've come back for you?"

"'Cause I told them not to, made 'em take a vow."

"Well, that ain't gonna help you, but I guess they got away, at least for now. Don't know if the army will keep lookin' for 'em."

Yeah, they did get away, and ain't nobody gonna find 'em where they went.

Beidler lay back against the trunk of a poplar. "You know, Dawkins, the thing I can't figure out about you is why a man would risk his neck to save a bunch of blue bellies out to catch him. Or why you returned our horses at the Missouri." Beidler shook his head. "You'd have been long gone by now if you hadn't been so foolish."

Dawkins just nodded and smiled. "I suppose you're right, Marshal." For a lawman, Beidler did not seem to understand much about loyalty and honor.

They ate another dreary meal of dried beef, crackers, and coffee. Beidler built up the fire and sat against a tree. Dawkins shivered in the evening air, wondering if the marshal would give him a bedroll, when a horse neighed along the trail. He looked over at Beidler, who was already staring beyond the fire toward the wagon road.

A few minutes later, they heard the clicking of horse hooves and then a youthful voice floating in the dark. "Hello, the camp, can I come in?"

Beidler rose, Colt in hand. "Who is it?"

Into the light of the fire strode a young soldier, tall and skinny with a mop of sandy-blond hair. "It's me, Marshal, Lieutenant Craft."

"Well, I'll be a son of a gun!" Beidler cried. "Look what the cat drug in. A day late and a dollar short."

Dawkins watched the young man he figured to be barely twenty grin and shake Beidler's hand.

"What the hell you doin' here, any damned way? I thought the army ordered you back to the Milk?"

"They did, they did, Marshal. But I talked Major Ilges at Fort Benton into a horse and permission to find you." Craft laughed. "I didn't want you to get all the credit for yourself."

Beidler pointed to the lieutenant's hand. "Looks like you healed up pretty well, must have been that doctorin' I gave you."

"Must have been," said Craft in a way that Dawkins thought not altogether sincere.

"Well, shoot, I don't know what happened to my manners." Beidler pointed toward Dawkins. "Here's the gentleman that set us afoot and led us on this merry chase. Meet Bill Dawkins."

Dawkins looked up at Craft, feeling about like he had passing all the folks around Missoula earlier in the day. But he was surprised to see a hint of interest and caring in the lieutenant's stare.

"That's the leader, then," said Craft. "What about the other two?"

"They got away." Beidler kicked the ground. "Most likely out of the territory by now."

Craft pointed toward his horses. "Give me a few minutes and I'll join you."

Beidler returned to the fire. "He's a good enough lad, I guess," he said in a low voice to Dawkins. "But green as the grass we're sittin' on." Beidler grinned. "He might be able to tell you somethin' about your lady friend, the doctor. She worked on him after we come aboard the *Chambers*." Beidler added wood to the fire. "I'd have caught up with you a lot sooner if I hadn't had to tote him along."

A little while later, Craft walked into the well-lit camp, carrying his saddle and bedroll. He placed his McClellan alongside

Beidler's gear and pulled an unopened bottle of whiskey from his saddlebags. "I was hoping we'd be having a celebration, Marshal."

Beidler snapped his head toward the liquor. "Hallelujah, Lieutenant. You finally done somethin' right. I got a terrible dry, didn't think I'd be having any liquor 'till we got to Helena."

Craft sat near the fire. "Shoot, no, we should have a drink. How do you put it? Let's irrigate."

Beidler dumped the coffee from his tin cup and greedily shoved it in Craft's direction. "Fill 'er up."

Dawkins watched the soldier fill Beidler's cup to the brim. The lawman drank, almost desperately, finishing before the young man could pour his own mug full. Craft refilled Beidler's cup and leaned against his saddle.

"Where are you taking this man, Marshal?"

"Territorial court in Helena." Beidler gulped the last of his whiskey and eyed Craft's bottle.

"Here have another," said Craft. "What charges are you preferring?"

"Horse stealin', attempted murder, aiding and abetting a fugitive of justice, and so forth," Beidler slurred. "This hoss is in a hell of a lot of trouble."

He staggered to his feet on wobbly legs. "Lieutenant, I got to go make water. Hold down the fort and keep your eyes on our prisoner." He stumbled into darkness.

Craft waited until Beidler left the campfire, and then tossed the whiskey from his cup into the fire. He raised a finger to his lips and winked at Dawkins.

When Beidler weaved his way back to the fire, Craft filled his own cup and nodded at the marshal. "Let's have another." He poured the little man more liquor. "What's next for you? I mean after you get this fella to Helena?"

"Probably rest up, and then take off for another outlaw." Beidler drank and shook his head. "Whew, boy, you brought the good stuff, didn't ya?"

"Oh, yes sir, this isn't trade whiskey," answered Craft. "I bought this at a fancy bar on Front Street in Fort Benton."

Dawkins's mind raced, watching Beidler drink heavily, egged on all the while by this pup of an officer. The young man feigned to partake in the drunk, but only sipped from his cup and dumped his liquor once more when Beidler stumbled to the edge of the camp again to relieve himself.

In less than an hour, the bottle was empty. With the exception of what little liquor Craft poured for himself, Beidler had finished an entire quart of whiskey.

The last thing Dawkins heard the marshal say before he collapsed on his bedroll was, "Lieutenant, give that Dawkins his bedroll, he behaved himself today…"

Craft fed the fire and pulled his watch. He looked down at Beidler, shaking his head. "That man's drinking is his Achilles's heel." He gingerly removed the marshal's pistol and tucked it in his belt. Then he ambled over to where Dawkins was chained and knelt close, whispering, "You're leaving here tonight." Craft unlocked the handcuffs. "Wait here, for now." He returned to Beidler and placed one of the cuffs around the lawman's wrist. "Don't worry, he's dead to the world," Craft said in full voice as he locked the other cuff to the pommel of Beidler's saddle.

Dawkins rubbed his wrists, stunned by his good fortune. All he could think to say was, "Why?"

"Let's just say it's recompense toward a debt I can never pay in full." Craft looked about the camp. "You need to ride now. Take my mare. It belongs to me; the other horse is the army's. You don't need any more trouble with us."

Dawkins rose, pointing toward the picketed mounts. "One of those is mine."

"Take them both, then, but hurry on, and don't stop till you're out of the territory."

Dawkins scurried about camp collecting his saddlebags, rifle, and other equipment Beidler had confiscated. The gold La Barge had given him was still in the bags along with his gunbelt, which he quickly buckled on. He saddled Craft's horse and organized his gear. It took more time to pack the second horse with all his worldly possessions. Within half an hour, he was ready to ride.

He walked back to the fire where Craft still stood, eyeing the drunken lawman. "About ready to head out?" asked the lieutenant.

"I reckon so, but what about you? What's gonna happen when he sobers up tomorrow?"

"There'll be hell to pay," said Craft as he turned away from the drunken lawman. "But I'll be all right. As for you, you're not a murderer or a horse thief." The lieutenant shook Dawkins's hand. "I know what you did for my squadron in that fight with the Sioux, and I understand now why that Miller boy attacked our man at Rock Creek."

Dawkins shook his head. "Adel?"

Craft nodded toward the two horses. "Best be moving, now."

Dawkins smiled and walked away. He turned when the lieutenant spoke once more. "Bill, tell her she's still my angel."

Beidler awoke long after the rising sun had burned away the dew on the river bottom. He was hot and kicked away the sweaty horse blanket thrown over his legs. He took a deep breath and stirred from his bed, trying to ignore a murderous headache. Half-asleep, he fell on his back when he reached the end of a chain that was locked around his chest. He shook his head violently and rubbed his eyes to clear his whiskey-blurred vision.

Squinting into the harsh glare of the morning sun, he saw a fresh fire but no one in the camp. He rolled on his belly and saw the chain was locked to a pine as big around as his leg. Turning back to the fire, he only glimpsed matted grass where he had chained Dawkins the night before. Beidler shook his head again, as if it might awaken him from this black dream, then bellowed, "Craft…Lieutenant Craft, where are you? You all right, boy? Can you hear me?"

Beidler breathed fast and shallow, trying to figure how he came to be chained to a tree with his prisoner—his prize—and his bona fides missing. Then he heard rustling outside of camp and Craft appeared across the fire and knelt to place a coffeepot near the coals.

"Craft," Beidler barked, spittle spraying from his mouth, "Where's Dawkins, and why the hell am I locked up?"

Craft set the pot on a flat rock, then took a seat on a fallen log. He looked Beidler in the eyes and shrugged his shoulders. "He's gone."

"I can see that, you idiot," snorted Beidler. "What'd he do? Get the jump on you after I went to sleep?"

"After you went to sleep?" mocked Craft. "You mean after you passed out, drunker than a skunk?"

Before Beidler could speak, Craft interrupted him. "I let Dawkins go, right after you went to sleep, Marshal." The young man looked toward the rising sun, well above the eastern horizon. "Best forget about that man, Marshal, he's long gone, probably halfway to Idaho by now."

"Damnation!" Beidler cried, pulling against the chain with both hands. Between his hangover and this turn of events, he could hardly think straight enough to speak.

"I knew it would go hard on you, Marshal, but I had to do it," said Craft. "I had to let him go."

"Have you lost your mind, boy?" asked Beidler, wild eyes staring upon the young soldier. "He was my prisoner, he was a horse thief. I'll have your tail for this. Now get me out of these chains." Beidler calculated he still might catch up with Dawkins if he left this instant. Take Craft's mounts, leave the fool on foot, and kill more horseflesh to recapture his man.

"It's not going to happen, Marshal," said Craft, as if he could read Beidler's mind. "We're going to stay in this camp for at least the rest of this day. You can relieve yourself off the side of your bed, there, and I'll make us some breakfast, but you're not going anywhere."

"Why!" bellowed Beidler. "Just tell me that."

"Because that man is not a criminal, and I don't trust your brand of justice to give him a fair treatment."

"It's that doctor on the *Chambers*!" hissed Beidler. "She put you up to this, didn't she?"

"No," said Craft, gently shaking his head. "But Dr. Johnston did help me see for myself how wrong and misguided this whole chase across the territory has been."

Beidler screamed, "That's a horse thief you just cut lose." He rubbed his face, then pounded the ground with both fists. "You unlock this chain or I'll see that you're court-martialed right out of the army, Craft."

Beidler was astonished to see Craft, that pup of an officer, just rub his chin and chuckle.

"As far as I know, Dawkins is no horse thief. I think you just lost our horses up north. All I know for sure is that Dawkins and the Millers found our mounts and left them on the river for us."

"Bull," hissed Beidler.

"Maybe, but that's my side of the story," said Craft with a slight grin. "That would be my testimony, that and you being too drunk to trust with the horses on your watch. Just think, everyone would know Marshal X. Beidler was outfoxed by a green shavetail. How would you ever salvage your reputation?"

"You know that's a lie, Craft. I wet-nursed you across most of Montana Territory. Saved you from the Sioux, starvation, and that rattlesnake bite. For everything I taught you, you're an ungrateful whelp."

"Well, Marshal," said Craft as he fetched the steaming coffeepot, "I did learn a lot from you. I figured out a lot on my own, too."

Beidler snorted, "Bah."

"Yes sir, I learned how it was Dawkins that saved us from the Sioux and that I nearly lost my hand on account of you dragging me across the prairie to catch the *Chambers*."

Before Beidler could speak, Craft went on. "Marshal, your days are numbered, just like the buffalo and those hostiles we fought. We don't need your brand of justice any longer. Maybe in the frontier days of the territory you served a purpose, but not now. It won't be long before Montana's a state, with regular courts and lawmen in every county." Craft tossed a stick toward Beidler when he turned away, trying to ignore the young man. "Marshal, I figured you're not that much different than a lot of the men you've chased and hung through the years. All you are is a bully with a badge, an outlaw turned inside out."

"Well, now I've heard it all." Beidler leaned against the pine in resignation and closed his eyes. Nearly fifty, he needed his job as a deputy marshal. He had no family, no real friends,

THE RIVER'S SONG

and no money to speak of. Without his position, he might end up swamping a saloon, telling stories for drinks and slops. If he did not play his cards right, he could die a penniless wretch.

"All right, Craft," he sighed. "We'll play it your way this time. But if you tell anyone how all this ended, I'll blow your brains out."

Craft placed a cup of steaming coffee near Beidler and retreated back to his log across the fire, as if Beidler might strike him like some kind of snake. "You don't have to worry about that, Marshal. I'm not after your reputation." He nodded to the west. "I just want to see an honest man free."

Chapter Twenty-five

Dawkins looked down upon the sprawling settlement of Seattle, wondering if a town could be built on any steeper terrain. The fall rain that had hounded him since he left Fort Walla Walla had subsided, and the rising sun revealed a cloudless sky. Even after Montana Territory, he was stunned by the setting. To the south, Mount Rainier loomed larger than any mountain he had ever seen. It was dusted by fresh snow and gleamed white and gold in the morning light. Ahead, Puget Sound was shrouded in a fog that hid the base of the Olympic Mountains beyond, covered in a purple blanket of timber.

For two weeks he had traveled the wagon road along the Yakima, the fall colors gaining in yellows, oranges, and reds with each passing day. Rain slowed him, causing him to tent here and there, waiting for breaks in the squalls that rolled in like waves from the west.

Dawkins no longer spied his back trail, as he had when crossing Lolo Pass into Idaho Territory. He had followed Lieutenant Craft's advice and made the border two days after gaining his freedom, traveling day and night. When he reached Idaho, he still guarded his rear and masked his camps all the way to Lewiston. After ten days of arduous travel in

THE RIVER'S SONG

mountainous terrain, he crossed a pass over the northern edge of the Blue Mountains and rode into Washington, feeling safe for the first time in months.

All told he spent thirty days on the trail, traveling close to six hundred miles. The promise of a new life with Adel sustained him every waking minute and in his dreams. Now that he was so close, it almost seemed unreal that they would be together by day's end.

Since Beidler had burned her letter, Dawkins had recited her words in his mind and opened her father's watch even when the time did not matter. Sometimes, when he was reminded of the marshal, he wondered about that young lieutenant who had freed him. He worried about Jim and Ezra, hoping they would soon write. He daydreamed about finding some enterprise they could all share in. But as Dawkins descended the hills above Seattle, he had only one thought on his mind, and he searched for First Providence Hospital on Madison Street.

Reaching the edge of town, he rode through small clearings and patches of spruce and fir. He smelled fresh-cut lumber and wood smoke. He thought it was Friday, or maybe Saturday, but too many folks traveled to work for a Sunday. He laughed, wondering if he would ever lose track of the days like that again.

Nearing the waterfront, he saw a fleet of steamers and frigates running about, hauling passengers and freight to other ports. Along the muddy streets, he found a hive of activity, with people unloading crates, barrels of liquor, chickens, tools, canned goods, beef, fresh fish, and everything else that made life easier. He spied a three-story, wooden building in the distance and inspected it with his field glasses. A cross rose from a tall cupola, and Dawkins made his way to the new hospital.

When he tied his two horses to a hitching post, his hands shook from excitement and nervousness. He strode up the steps and entered through two wide doors. He was startled by a life-sized statue of a saint staring at him from across the entrance room. So much so that he did not notice a young nun sitting behind a desk near the wall to his right. He nearly jumped out of his boots when she cheerfully said, "Good morning, sir. I'm Sister Katherine, may I help you?"

Dawkins smiled. "Yes ma'am, ah, Sister Katherine, good mornin'." He thought the young woman was only in her teens, but with all but her face covered in a black habit, it was hard to tell. "I'm looking for one of your doctors, Dr. Johnston?"

Sister Katherine nodded and rubbed her forehead. "She's caring for the sick this morning at the County Poor Farm, south of town."

"I see." Dawkins considered whether to ask for directions or return later.

"Perhaps someone else could see you, sir?"

"Oh, I'm sorry, no, I'm not ill. I'm a friend of the doctor's."

Sister Katherine quietly giggled and then blushed. "Oh, my," she said, covering her mouth. Then she smiled. "My goodness, are you Bill Dawkins?"

"Yes, I am." Dawkins shared a laugh with the young nun. He noticed her eyes welling with tears.

"This is going to be the happiest day of her life, Mr. Dawkins—"

"Please, call me Bill, my papa was Mr. Dawkins."

"Well, sir, she's been worried sick about you, ever since she received a letter from the Miller brothers."

"They wrote already?" Dawkins was overcome with relief. He felt as if a weight had been lifted from his shoulders. "Where did they end up, then?"

"Adel got the letter earlier in the week, from Westbridge," said Sister Katherine.

More people entered the hospital, and the young nun greeted them and turned to Dawkins. "Adel will be back here around midday, maybe three o'clock or so. I can't wait to tell her you're here."

Dawkins asked for a sheaf of paper and pencil. He scribbled a note and folded the paper. "Sister Katherine, it was my pleasure to meet you. Please give this to Adel and tell her I'll be back by three."

Adel bounced back and forth as the horse-drawn mud wagon returned her and the other staff to the hospital. Some of the nurses chatted and laughed, but she gazed out the open window toward the deep blue water of Puget Sound. The last two weeks had been a blur of new places, people, and work.

Her first task after arriving in Seattle had been to break off her engagement with George. She returned his engagement ring, placing it in his hand and telling him it was no fault of his that she had changed her mind. He asked if there was someone else, and she told him the truth.

Her position at the hospital and the County Poor Farm helped occupy her worried mind. She met the other doctors, all men, and the nurses and nuns who made the place of healing run like a tight ship. And she became friends with Sister Katherine, the young nun who gladly shared her room.

Adel was enthralled with her work but lonely in the busy little city. At night in the sparse quarters the hospital staff had temporarily provided her, she told Sister Katherine, or Sister Katy, as she called her in private, all about her hopes and dreams for a life with a man wanted by the law and the army in Montana Territory. Sister Katy listened with a wide-eyed stare as Adel told her how handsome and considerate he was. Adel told Sister Katy how he had saved her from wild Indians and a loveless marriage.

Adel had known she would beat Bill to Seattle. She thought he would be along, though, within a few days of her arrival. After two weeks, she began to worry and think the worst, and then the letter arrived from Ezra Miller. He and Jim had safely reached Canada after running from Marshal Beidler, who caught up with them no more than thirty miles from the Idaho border. They only escaped because Bill stayed behind to slow the marshal. They were eager to return to the United States and awaited word of Bill's arrival.

Nearing the hospital on busy Fifth Avenue, Adel prayed again for Bill's safety and a happy reunion. Leaving the stage, she calmed her nerves and walked quickly to the hospital entrance. On Saturday afternoon, she was off-duty after her work at the County Poor Farm, but she wanted to see Sister Katy and visit an elderly patient she did not expect to survive a recent heart seizure.

When Adel met Sister Katy's eyes in the entrance room, something told her this was the day she had begun to fear might never come to be. The young nun rose from her desk and squeezed both of Adel's hands. "He's here!" She glanced left and right, then whispered, "He left you a note."

Adel was so light-headed and dizzy with excitement and happiness she thought she might faint. "Where is it?"

Sister Katy looked down at the floor. "I lost it." Then she laughed and pulled a folded piece of paper from the pocket of her habit.

Adel frantically unfolded the note and read the few words quickly to herself.

"You've just got to tell me what he wrote," Sister Katy pleaded.

THE RIVER'S SONG

"Dear Adel, by the grace of God and Lieutenant Craft I made it. Forever yours, Bill."

The little nun hugged Adel and whispered, "I told him to come back at three."

Dawkins felt clean for the first time since departing the *Chambers*. After leaving the hospital, he stabled his two horses and kicked about town. Visiting a barbershop, he enjoyed a shave and a haircut. Dawkins availed himself of the hot bath in the back, washing away weeks of dust, sweat, and fear. Then he changed into new clothes he had bought at a haberdashery and found a Chinese laundry to wash his trail-worn duds. He inspected himself in a storefront mirror. Set off with new boots and belt, the light gray wool suit against a white shirt and black string tie looked pretty smart. He kept his old felt hat, though, giving a bit of character to his outfit. Looking once more at his image, Dawkins thought, *I look like a man about to get married.*

He pulled his watch, Adel's father's watch, and checked the time. In his other vest pocket, he felt for the reassuring bulge of a gold wedding band. With another hour to kill, he walked down to the pier at the end of Madison Street, a few blocks below the hospital.

The sky had stayed clear, as the morning promised, and he strolled along the wooden deck, listening to gulls crying overhead and waves lapping against the pilings below. Reaching the end of the pier, he leaned against the railing and gazed across the purple depths to the Olympic Mountains. Pretty far for a Pennsylvania farm boy to have come, by way of a bloody war, the Missouri River, Montana Territory, and a thousand-mile chase. This felt like a place to make a home, though, with the right woman. He closed his eyes and breathed the sea-laden air. Then he heard familiar steps and the voice of an angel.

"Bill! Bill!" When he turned, Adel was nearly in his arms, tears falling as she rushed toward him. "You made it, thank God, you made it!"

He just got a glimpse of her pretty face, her long brown hair and doe eyes before they embraced. He held her lithesome body, smelled her perfume, and heard the words they spoke while he felt carried outside himself and suspended from above. Then he kissed her, and every worry, every loss, every sadness drifted away like the words to the river's song.

THE END

Acknowledgments

I am indebted to Dennis Foley and the Authors of the Flathead for endless patience and encouragement. Debbie Burke has diligently taught a scientist to write fiction. Andrew McKean, Mike Korn, Tom Peck, Ron Aasheim, and Carol Buchanan reviewed manuscripts and excerpts, providing helpful suggestions and edits.

About the Author

Jim Satterfield is a wildlife biologist and has lived in Northeastern Montana for five years. He has a great love of the Missouri Breaks and has walked the same ground Sitting Bull's renegade Lakota traveled and hunted. Satterfield is a recipient of the Pacific Northwest Writers Association 2011 Zola Award for historical fiction. *The River's Song* is his first novel.

Made in the USA
Lexington, KY
20 November 2012